"We may run into trouble if someone works up the guts to challenge me."

We? This bizarre conversation had her bewildered. Us against them. Did he imagine she'd be happy to be one of those stoop-shouldered, timid, obedient women?

Or... Leah replayed everything he'd said. His expressions, subtle though they were. His actions, if it was true he'd left the hideout key to the car deliberately to give her a chance to get away. His care with her injuries, the flickers of rage she'd seen. Even when she fought, when she hurt him, he'd still been careful not to hurt her.

Very slowly, she said, "You're not one of them, are you?"

THE LAST RESORT

USA TODAY Bestselling Author

JANICE KAY JOHNSON

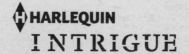

HARLEQUIN
INTRIGUE

For Barb, a great editor and even better friend,
and for her faithful sidekick, Panda.

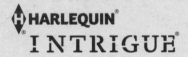

Recycling programs
for this product may
not exist in your area.

ISBN-13: 978-1-335-13692-3

The Last Resort

Copyright © 2020 by Janice Kay Johnson

This edition published by arrangement with Harlequin Books S.A.

For questions and comments about the quality of this book,
please contact us at CustomerService@Harlequin.com.

Harlequin Enterprises ULC
22 Adelaide St. West, 40th Floor
Toronto, Ontario M5H 4E3, Canada
www.Harlequin.com

Printed in U.S.A.

An author of more than ninety books for children and adults with more than seventy-five for Harlequin, **Janice Kay Johnson** writes about love and family, and pens books of gripping romantic suspense. A *USA TODAY* bestselling author and an eight-time finalist for the Romance Writers of America RITA® Award, she won a RITA® Award in 2008. A former librarian, Janice raised two daughters in a small town north of Seattle, Washington.

Books by Janice Kay Johnson

Harlequin Intrigue

Hide the Child
Trusting the Sheriff
Within Range
Brace for Impact
The Hunting Season
The Last Resort

Visit the Author Profile page at Harlequin.com.

CAST OF CHARACTERS

Leah Keaton—Captured by a vicious militia group, she attempts to escape—and fails. Nobody gives *her* a choice when she's "claimed" by a member of the group. How can she fall in love with a man who *says* he's one of the good guys...but may be lying?

Spencer Wyatt—An FBI agent working undercover in a domestic terrorism investigation, he's within weeks of being able to stop a high-profile attack on the US government. Will he blow this whole investigation to protect one innocent woman? His conscience and his heart bump up against his need to finish the job.

Edward Higgs—A former US Air Force colonel, he turns his rage at being forced to take early retirement into a war to shake up America...and return to the days when white men ran the country, women did what they were told and borders kept out the undesirables.

Joe Osenbrock—Recruited by Higgs, Joe bitterly resents Spencer, the man who has become second in command. A challenge to hand-to-hand combat will allow him to prove himself—and take Spencer's woman.

Dirk Ritchie—A weak link in the militia, he's the one man who can bring down the undercover agent betraying them all. But will he?

Chapter One

Leah Keaton eased up on the gas pedal too late to prevent her right front tire from dropping into an epic pothole with a distinct *clunk*. She winced.

Along with a gradual rise in elevation, the road was getting narrower, the dense northwest forest reclaiming it. The roots from vast Douglas fir, spruce and cedar trees created a corrugated effect as they crumbled the pavement. Long, feathery limbs occasionally brushed the sides of her modest sedan. Pale lichen draped from branches. Thick clumps of ferns and wiry branches of what might be berries overhung the edges of the pavement.

Her mother could have been right, that this was a wasted and even unwise journey.

All of which was assuming, Leah thought ruefully, that she hadn't taken a wrong turn. In her distant memory, a carved and painted wood sign had marked the turnoff to her great-uncle's rustic resort in the north Cascade Mountains, not that far from the Canadian border. She reminded herself this was rain forest, which by definition meant wood rotted quickly. Once the sign fell, moss and forest under-growth would have hidden it in a matter of weeks.

Forcing herself to loosen her grip on the steering wheel, Leah caught a glimpse of Mount Baker above the treetops. At not quite eleven thousand feet in elevation, Baker wasn't the largest of the string of volcanoes that stretched from California to the Canadian border, but it was plenty imposing anyway with year-round snow and ice cloaking the mountain flanks. Leah remembered from when she was a kid seeing puffs of steam escaping vents at the summit, a reminder that Mount Baker still had the potential to erupt.

Weirdly, the memory relaxed her. This road felt familiar. If she was right, it would soon climb more sharply yet above a river carrying seasonal snowmelt that ultimately joined the larger North Fork Nooksack River. As a child, she'd hated the drive home from the resort because the edge was so close to the road, the drop-off so precipitous. She hadn't trusted the rusting guardrail at all.

What if a tumultuous spring had undercut the cliff and the road no longer went all the way to the resort?

The tires of her car crunched onto gravel as the pavement ended. She had to go slower yet, because potholes and ruts made the way even more perilous.

Although he'd closed the resort something like fifteen years ago, Uncle Edward had continued living here until his death last fall. Had he really not minded navigating this road when he had to stock up on groceries? According to Leah's mother, he'd declared flatly, "This is home," and remained undaunted by the perils of living in such an isolated location as an old man.

"Stubborn as that old coot Harry Truman, who wouldn't evacuate when Mount St. Helens blew," Mom had grumbled, mentioning the name of a rugged individual who'd refused to leave the mountainside before the volcano erupted in 1980. "He'll end the same way. You just wait and see."

Leah's dad had gently pointed out that, despite being in his nineties, Uncle Edward hadn't displayed even a hint of dementia and therefore was fully capable of making his own decisions. Dad had shaken his head. "He's lived up there most of his life. Imagine what it would be like for him to move to a senior apartment with busybody neighbors all around and traffic going by night and day."

"But we could find him a nice—" Mom had broken off, knowing she'd lost the argument. She just didn't understand her uncle, who'd spent his entire life in the north Cascade Mountains.

She did understand why he'd left the resort to Leah, the only one of his nieces and nephews who had genuinely loved vacations spent at the remote resort. Leah would have been happy to spend every summer there—at least until teenage hormones struck and hanging out with friends at home became a priority—but her mother refused to let her stay beyond their annual two-week family vacations spent in one of the lakeside cabins.

The road started to seriously climb, blue sky

ahead. A minute later she saw the small river to the left, water tumbling over boulders and pausing in deep pools. This was July, the height of the melt-off on the mountain above. By fall, the water level would lower until barely a creek ran between rocky banks.

She stayed close to the steep bank on the right. After sneaking a few peeks at the guardrail in places it had crumpled or even disappeared, she decided she just might do the same thing coming down. It wasn't as if she was likely to meet any oncoming traffic, for heaven's sake. She could drive on whatever side of the road she wanted. And, while she'd brought a suitcase, sleeping bag and enough food to hold her for a night or two, she knew the old resort buildings might be so decrepit she'd have no choice but to turn right around and head back down the mountain. Uncle Edward had been ninety-three when he died. He wasn't likely to have done any significant maintenance in many years.

Still…the location was great, the view of Mount Baker across a shallow lake and an alpine meadow spectacular. There'd even been a glimpse of the more distant Mount Shuksan, too. Backed by national forest, the land alone had to be worth something, didn't it? She hoped Uncle Edward hadn't envisioned her building up the resort again and running it; despite good memories of the stays here, she'd grown up in Portland, Oregon, gone to college in southern California. Wilderness girl, she wasn't.

Learning about the inheritance had given her hope. She'd been dreaming of going back to school to become a veterinarian. The cost was one factor in her hesitation. Animal doctors didn't make the kind of income people doctors did, but finished four years of graduate school with the same load of debt.

Never having dreamed Uncle Edward would leave the resort to her, she couldn't help feeling as if he'd somehow known what it would mean to her.

To her relief, the road curved away from the river and plunged back into the forest. Leah's anticipation rose as she peered ahead through the tunnel formed by the enormous old evergreen trees.

It was another ten minutes before her car popped out into the grassy meadow, spangled with wild-flowers, and there was the resort.

Except…there were already people here. Her foot went to the brake. Half a dozen—no, more than that—SUVs were parked in front of the lodge and cabins. Not a single car, she noted in a corner of her mind. These all looked like the kind of vehicles de-signed to drive on icy pavement and even off-road.

This was weird, but…she'd come this far. Surely, there was a legitimate reason for people to be here.

After a moment she continued forward, coasting to a stop in front of the lodge. Head turning, she saw that some of the cabins had been repaired in the re-cent past. Several new roofs and the raw wood of new porches and window frames were unmistakable.

A woman on one of those porches looked startled at the sight of her and slipped back inside the cabin, maybe to tell someone else about the arrival of a stranger.

Two men appeared around the corner of the lodge, probably having heard her car engine.

Who *were* these people? Had Mom been wrong, and Uncle Edward had kept the resort open? But still, he'd died eight months ago. Could he have sold it, with no one knowing?

She'd braked and put the gear in Park, but unease stilled her hand before she turned the key.

What if—? But she'd hesitated too long. The men had reached her car, their expressions merely inquiring. There had to be a reasonable explanation. She should be glad the resort buildings hadn't begun to tumble down.

In the sudden silence after she shut off the engine, the car keys bit into her hand. Taking a deep breath, Leah unbuckled her seat belt, opened the door and got out.

One of the men, gray-haired but as fit as a younger man, smiled. "You must be lost."

The muscular guy behind him had full-sleeve tattoos bared below a muscle-hugging tan T-shirt. And…could that be a holstered pistol at his waist?

Dear God, yes.

Say yes. Claim you were heading anywhere else. Let them give you directions and then drive away.

She could go to the nearest small town—Glacier, population 211—and ask about the group staying here. There was only one highway in and out of this area. These people had driven here. They'd have been noticed.

But the older of the two men looked friendly, not hostile at all. There'd be a logical explanation.

"No, actually," she said. "Um… I own this resort."

His smile fell away. "You're the *owner*?"

"That's right. I inherited the place from my great-uncle, Edward Preston."

Outwardly, the man relaxed. "Oh, we've been wondering what was going to happen to the place. The old man let us mostly take over the resort these past few summers in exchange for working on it. We had no idea he'd died until we got here in late June and found it empty."

"Didn't you ask in Glacier or Maple Falls? Surely, people there knew he'd died."

"Some bed-and-breakfast owner I talked to said she hadn't heard anything." He nodded toward the lodge. "Why don't you come on in and we can talk? I don't know about you, but I could use a cup of coffee."

Conscious of the other man's eyes boring into her, she hesitated again, but what else could she do but say, "Sure. Thanks. I'd forgotten what a long drive it is to get up here."

The pair flanked her as they started toward the lodge, which sounded deceptively grand. The old log building only had six guest rooms, all upstairs, a large kitchen and living space and the owner's small apartment at the back. Mostly, Uncle Edward had rented out the ten cabins. What guests he'd allowed to stay in the lodge understood they had to bring their own food and cook for themselves. "Not like I'm going to wait on them hand and foot," he'd snorted.

Leah became nervously aware that several other men had stepped out of cabins, their gazes on her.

Most wore camo cargo pants, as did the so-far silent man walking to her right. None of them called out. Their appraisal felt…cold.

She was imagining things. They were curious, that was all.

Only…why weren't there other women? Children?

The porch steps were solid, having obviously been replaced. The older man opened the front door and they ushered her in. *Herded me in*, that uneasy voice inside her head whispered.

She did smell coffee. In fact, a couple of empty cups sat on the long plank table where guests had eaten or sat around in the evening to play board games or poker.

"Let me get that coffee," the gray-haired man said. "You want sugar? I have milk but no cream."

"Milk's fine. Just a dash, and a teaspoon of sugar."

"Coming right up. Have a seat." He nodded toward the benches to each side of the table.

Knowing she'd feel trapped once she was sitting with her feet under the table, she strolled instead toward the enormous river-rock fireplace where she had once upon a time roasted marshmallows for s'mores.

None of the men she'd seen thus far looked as if they'd do anything that frivolous. Chew sixteen-gauge steel nails, maybe. Graham crackers, gooey charred marshmallows and melted chocolate? Hard to picture.

The silent guy remained standing, a shoulder against the log wall right beside the door out to the porch. He watched her steadily.

Maybe he'd be friendly if she was. But before she

could think of anything to say that wasn't too inane, the older man returned from the kitchen with a cup of coffee in each hand.

He glanced toward the second man but didn't offer to fetch him a cup, too.

Leah didn't feel as if she had any choice but to go back to the table and sit down.

He took a sip before asking, "Mind telling me your plans?"

"Um… I wanted to see what condition the buildings were in. And, well, probably I'll sell the place."

"Sell it, huh? You have a price in mind?"

"I have no idea what land is worth up here." If it was worth anything. She had to be honest with herself. "Are you interested?"

"Could be. We'd hate having to relocate."

Feeling and sounding timid, she asked, "Do you mind telling me what you're doing up here? I'm assuming you're not all vacationing here three months a year."

The flicker of amusement in his eyes wasn't at all reassuring. He thought she was funny. Naive.

"No," he said thoughtfully. "No, this is a business."

More unnerved by the minute, she gripped the handle of the mug. She could buy herself time by throwing hot coffee in one of the men's faces if she had to run for it.

Just then, the front door opened and two more men walked in. Cool gazes assessed her. One of them raised dark eyebrows as he looked at the man acting as host. Leah had no trouble hearing the unspoken question.

Who the hell is she and what does she want?

One of the newcomers was short and stocky with sandy hair. Sort of Dennis the Menace, with the emphasis on *menace*.

The other was formidable enough to scare her more. Eyes a crystalline gray could have been chips of ice. Tanned and dark-haired, he had the kind of shoulders that suggested he did some serious weight lifting.

And, dear God, both men wore holstered handguns at their waists.

Paramilitary was the word that came to mind. What had she walked into?

Be up front, she decided.

"I'm starting to feel a little uncomfortable," she said, focusing on the older man who almost had to be the leader of this bunch. "Why don't I head back to Glacier and find a room for the night? I'll talk to a real estate agent, and if you'd like you can come down tomorrow, meet me for lunch, maybe. We can talk."

Still appearing relaxed, he said slowly, "That might work. Ah…in answer to your earlier question, what we do is run paintball camps. It's mostly men who come up here. They immerse themselves in the wilderness and harmless war games, have a hell of a good time. We've built up a serious seasonal business. Like I said, finding another location anywhere near as perfect as this one would be next to impossible."

Because this land was so remote. Leah had to wonder whether it was true Uncle Edward had let them use his place for several summers in a row, or whether they'd somehow heard he had died and moved in under the assumption no one would be interested enough in a falling-down resort in the middle of nowhere to bother checking on it.

She stole another look at the three men on their feet, now ranged around the room. "Those...look like real guns."

Boss Man across from her shrugged. "Sure, we have a shooting range set up. A bunch of us have been out there all morning. Gotta keep sharp, even if we're mostly using paintball guns."

Nobody else's expression changed.

"Well," she said, starting to push herself up.

The sound of the back door opening was as loud as a shot. Bounced off the wall, she diagnosed, in a small, calm part of her mind surrounded by near hysteria.

All of the men turned their heads.

Grinning, a man emerged from the kitchen. Over his shoulder, he carried a *huge* gun, painted army green. Even as he said, "Hot damn!" before seeing her, Leah's blood chilled.

She'd seen pictures, taken in places like the Ukraine and Afghanistan. That wasn't a gun—it was a rocket launcher.

SON OF A BITCH.

Spencer Wyatt restrained himself from so much as twitching a muscle only from long practice. His mind worked furiously, though. Could this juxtaposition be any more disastrous? An unsuspecting woman wandering in here like a dumb cow to slaughter, coupled with that cocky, careless jackass Joe Osenbrock striding in with an effing *rocket launcher* over his shoulder? *Yee haw.*

Especially a young, pretty woman. Did she have any idea what trouble she was in?

Flicking a glance at her, he thought, yeah, she had a suspicion.

In fact, she said, in a voice that sounded a little too cheerful to be real, "Is that one of the paintball guns? I've never seen one before."

Good try.

Ed Higgs didn't buy it. "You know better than that. Damn. I wish I could let you go, but I can't."

She flung her full coffee cup at his face, leaped off the bench and tore for the front door, still standing ajar. Smart move, trying to get out of here. She actually brushed Spencer. He managed to look surprised and stagger back to give her a chance. No surprise, the little creep Larson was on her before she so much as touched the door.

She screamed and struggled. Her nails raked down Larson's cheek. Teeth set, he slammed her against the wall, flattening his body on hers. Spencer wanted to rip the little pissant off and throw *him* into the wall. Went without saying that he stayed right where he was. There was no way for him to help now that wouldn't derail his mission.

He had more lives than hers to consider.

Ed snapped, "Get her car keys. Wyatt, go over the car. When you're done, bring in her purse and whatever else she brought with her. Make sure you don't miss anything. Hear me?"

"Sure thing." He knew that once he had the keys, he'd have to hand them over to Higgs, who kept all the vehicle keys hidden away. No one had access to an SUV without Higgs knowing.

Arne Larson burrowed a hand into the woman's jeans pocket. When he groped with exaggerated pleasure, his captive struck quick as a snake, sinking her teeth into his shoulder. Arne yanked out the set of keys and backhanded her across the face. Her head snapped back, hitting the log wall with an audible *thunk*.

Spencer jerked but once again pulled hard on the leash. If she would only cooperate, she might have a chance to get out of this alive.

Arne tossed the keys at him and Spencer caught them. Without a word, he walked out, taking with him a last glimpse of her face, fine-boned and very pale except for the furious red staining her right jaw and cheek where the blow had fallen.

She hadn't locked the car, which didn't appear to be a rental. He used the keys to unlock the trunk and pull out a small wheeled suitcase, sized to be an airline carry-on, as well as a rolled-up sleeping bag and a cardboard box filled with basic food. Then he searched the trunk, removing the jack and spare tire, going through a bag of tools and an inadequate first-aid kit.

He couldn't believe even Higgs, with his paranoid

worldview, would think the woman in there was an undercover FBI or ATF agent.

She hadn't packed like one, he discovered, after opening the suitcase on the trunk lid once he closed it. Toiletries—she liked handmade soap, this bar smelling like citrus and some spice—jeans, T-shirts, socks and sandals. Two books, one a romance, one nonfiction about the Lipizzaner horses during World War II. He fanned the pages. Nothing fell out. A hooded sweatshirt. Lingerie, practical but pretty, too, lacking lace but skimpy enough to heat a man's blood and in brighter colors than he'd have expected from her.

Not liking the direction his thoughts had taken him, he dropped the mint-green bra back on top of the mess he'd made of the suitcase's contents.

There was nothing but food in the carton, including basics like boxes of macaroni and cheese, a jar of instant coffee, a loaf of whole-grain bread and packets of oatmeal with raisins. The sleeping bag, unrolled, unzipped and shaken, hid no secrets.

A small ice chest sat on the floor in front. No surprises there, either, only milk, several bars of dark chocolate, a tub of margarine and several cans of soda.

He took her purse from the passenger seat and dumped the contents out on the hood of the car. A couple of items rolled off. Plastic bottle of ibuprofen and a lip gloss. Otherwise, she carried an electronic reader, phone, a wallet, hairbrush, checkbook, wad of paper napkins, two tampons and some crumpled receipts for gas and meals. Her purse was a lot neater than most he'd seen.

Opening the wallet, he took out her driver's license first. Issued by the state of Oregon, it said her name was Leah E. Keaton. She was described as blond, which he'd dispute, but he didn't suppose strawberry blond would fit on the license. Weight, one hundred and twenty pounds, height, five feet six inches. Eyes, hazel. Age, thirty-one. Birthday, September 23.

She'd smiled for the photo. For a moment Spencer's eyes lingered. DMV photos were uniformly bad, no better than mug shots, but he saw hope and dignity in that smile. She reminded him of a time when his purpose wasn't so dark.

Did Leah E. Keaton know it wasn't looking good for her to make it to that next birthday, no matter what he did?

Chapter Two

Leah watched out the small window in an upstairs guest room with fury and fear as one of those brutes dug through her purse. He'd already searched her suitcase; it still lay open on the trunk of the car, the scant amount of clothing she'd brought left in a disheveled heap.

Everything that had been in her purse sat atop the hood. She felt stripped bare, increasing her shock. They would now know her name, her weight, that she used tampons. Her credit cards and checkbook were in their possession, along with her keys and phone.

That wasn't all. They had her, too.

Wyatt, if that was really his name, stood for a moment with his head bent, staring at the stuff he'd dumped out of her bag, before he began scooping it up and dropping it unceremoniously back in. Then he systematically examined the car interior, under the seats, the glove compartment, the cubbies designed to hold CDs, maps or drinks.

Following orders, of course.

Still gripped by fear, she saw him lie down on his

back and push himself beneath the undercarriage. Looking for a bomb? Or a tracking device? Leah had no idea.

Her heart cramped when he shifted toward the rear of the car. How could he miss seeing the magnetic box holding a spare key?

From this angle, there was no way to tell if he pocketed it.

Eventually, if her parents didn't hear from her, they'd sound the alarm and a county deputy might drive up here looking for her, but that wouldn't happen for days. Maybe as much as a week. She'd been vague about how long she intended to stay, and they knew she was unlikely to have phone service once she reached the rugged country tucked in the Cascade Mountain foothills.

Would these men kill a lone deputy who walked into the same trap she had?

When the man below climbed to his feet and closed her suitcase, she took a step back from the small-paned window. He didn't so much as glance upward as he carried the suitcase and her purse toward the lodge, disappearing beneath the porch roof. The groceries, ice chest and sleeping bag sat abandoned beside her car.

A rocket launcher. Or was it even a missile launcher? Was there a difference? The image flashed into her mind again. Leah tried to absorb the horror. Her knees gave out and she sagged to sit on the bed, fixing her unseeing gaze on the log walls with crumbled chinking. She wasn't naive enough not to

be aware that, with enough money and the right con-
nections, anybody could acquire military-grade and
banned weapons. But…what did these people intend
to *do* with this one? And what other weapons did
they have?

Her cheekbone throbbed. When she lifted her hand
to it, she winced. The swelling was obvious at even
a light touch. By tomorrow, a dark bruise would dis-
color half her face and probably crawl under her eye,
too. Her head ached.

Leah wished she could hold on to hope that, whatever the group's political objective, the men might
follow some standards of honor where women
were concerned. After the stocky blond guy who'd
slammed her against the wall had leered and tried to
grope her while his hand was in her pocket, that was
a no-go. Not one of the other men present had shown
the slightest reaction.

But she was sure she'd seen a woman on the porch
of one of the cabins. If women belonged to the group,
would they shrug at seeing another woman raped?
Somehow, she had trouble picturing this particular
group of men seeing any woman as an equal, though.
Armed to the teeth, buff, tattooed and cold-eyed, they
made her think of some of the far-right militia who
appeared occasionally on the news. Every gathering
she'd ever seen of white supremacists seemed to be
all male. If they had women here, they might be no
more willing than she was.

But maybe…this group had a completely different

objective. Could they be police or, well, members of some kind of super-secret military unit?

That thought didn't seem to offer an awful lot of hope.

Nausea welling, Leah pressed a hand to her stomach and moaned. She'd driven right into their midst, offering herself up like…like a virgin sacrifice. Except for not being a virgin. Somehow, she didn't think they'd care about that part, not if their leader decided to let them have her.

No one would be coming for her. She had to escape. Would they leave her in this room, the exit guarded? Feed her? Talk to her? Give her back any of her things?

Not her keys, that was for sure. She'd have to take the chance that Wyatt had missed the spare key. If not, she'd rather be lost and alone in the dense northwest rain forest miles from any other habitation than captive here. It would get cold at night, but this was July. She wouldn't freeze to death. At least she had sturdy athletic shoes on her feet instead of the sandals she'd also brought. Thank goodness she'd thrown on a sweatshirt over her tee.

The idea of driving at breakneck speed down the steep gravel road running high above the river scared her almost as much as those men did, but given a chance, she'd do it. If she got any kind of head start, she might be able to reach the paved stretch. Along there, she could look for a place to pull the car off the road and hide.

The hand still flattened on her stomach trembled.

Great plan. If, if, if. Starting with, *if* she could get out of this room. *If* she could escape the lodge. *If*...

No, at least she knew she could escape the room. For what good that would do, given that she'd still have to pop out in the hall where a guard would presumably be stationed.

Footsteps followed by voices came from right outside her door. Her head shot up.

AT WAR WITH HIMSELF, Spencer sat at the long table with a cup of coffee. Other men came and went, buzzing with excitement. They liked the idea of a captive, particularly a female. They were eager to see her. Only four of the guys had brought women with them, and they weren't sharing. Wasn't like the single guys could go into town one evening and pick up a woman at a bar. For one thing, Spencer hadn't noticed any bars or taverns any closer than Bellingham. The only exception, in Maple Falls, had obviously gone out of business. Higgs didn't let them leave the "base" anyway.

Their great leader had gone upstairs a minute ago. If he didn't reappear soon, Spencer would follow him. He thought Higgs intended to bring Leah Keaton downstairs. Let her have a bite to eat, try to soothe her into staying passive. The way she'd sunk her teeth into Larson's flesh, Spencer wasn't optimistic that passive was in her nature, but maybe she'd be smart enough to pretend. He was screwed if she didn't—unless he kept his eye on the goal and accepted that there were frequently collateral losses—

and this time, she'd be one of them. Except, he wasn't sure he could accept that.

Footsteps.

He took a long swallow of coffee and looked as if idly toward the woman Higgs led into the big open space.

She'd come along under her own power, without Higgs having to drag or shove her. If she had any brains, she was scared to death, but her face didn't show that. Instead, it was set, pale…and viciously bruised.

Spencer's temper stirred, but he stamped down on it.

"Have a seat." Higgs sounded almost genial.

Leah Keaton's gaze latched longingly on to her purse, sitting at one end of the table. Wouldn't make a difference for her to grab it; Higgs had taken the keys and probably her phone, which wouldn't do her any good anyway, not here.

"Dinner close to ready?" Higgs asked.

The wives and girlfriends were required to do the cooking and KP. Spencer had heard a couple of them come in the back door a while ago. Soon after, good smells had reached him.

Tim Fuller leaned against the wall right outside the kitchen to keep an eye on his wife, who was the best cook of the lot. Now he wordlessly stepped into the kitchen and came out to say, "Ten minutes. Spaghetti tonight."

Higgs smiled. "Sounds good. That'll give us all a chance to settle down, talk this over."

Leah sat with her back straight, her head bent so she could gaze down at her hands, clasped in front of her on the plank tabletop. Her expression didn't change an iota. Higgs's eyes lingered on her face, but he didn't comment.

Spencer continued to sip his coffee and hold his silence.

Eventually, Shelley Galt, thirty-two though she looked a decade older, brought out silverware and plates, then pitchers of beer and glasses. She kept her gaze down and her shoulders hunched as though she expected a blow at any moment. Spencer wanted to tell Shelley to steal her husband's car keys and run for it the next chance she had, but he knew better than to waste his breath even if that wouldn't have been stepping unacceptably out of his role. Shelley had married TJ Galt when she was seventeen. She probably didn't know any different or better.

Spencer had read and memorized her background, just as he had that of every single person expected to join them up here. He wasn't a trusting man.

The food came out on big platters, some carried by Jennifer Fuller, and the remaining members of the group filtered in, the men almost without exception eyeing Leah lasciviously. The four women were careful not to make eye contact with her.

Leah shook her head at the beer but took a can of soda—one, he suspected, from her own ice chest—and allowed Ed Higgs to dish up for her.

You can lead a horse to water, Spencer thought… but this one was smart enough to drink. And eat. She understood that starving herself wouldn't accomplish a damn thing.

Higgs tried to start a few conversations, earning him startled looks from his crew. He didn't do any better with Leah, who didn't react to any comments directed her way. What did he think she'd say to gems like, "Spectacular country here. Your uncle was smart to hold on to the land."

She blinked at that one but didn't look up.

Only when they were done and he said, "I need to talk to Ms. Keaton," did Spencer see her shoulders get even stiffer. "Wyatt," Higgs said, "you stay. You, too, Metz."

Rick Metz was an automaton, following orders without question, whatever they were. He carried the anger they all shared, but kept a lid on it. He rarely reacted even to jibes from the other guys. Spencer didn't see him raping a woman just because he could, which allowed him to relax infinitesimally.

Grumbles carried to Spencer, but none were made until the men stepped out onto the porch. If Higgs heard them, he offered no indication. Among this bunch, rebellion brewed constantly. Metz might be the only one who wanted to be given orders to carry out. The others accepted them, maybe seeing dimly that Ed Higgs, a former US Air Force colonel, was smarter than they were, his leadership essential to their accomplishing their hair-raising intentions. He reminded them constantly of his military service, happiest when the men called him Colonel. Compliance didn't mean they didn't seethe at the necessity and bitterly resent the inner knowledge that they were lesser in some way than Higgs. Spencer took advantage of that ever-brewing resentment when he could, giving a nudge here and there, inciting outbursts that had helped him climb to second- or third-in-command.

Once the other men were gone, Higgs said into the silence, "No reason for you to be afraid."

Leah did raise her head at that, not hiding her disbelief.

"We only need a couple more months. You'll have to stay with us that long. Once we're ready to move, you can go on your way."

A couple more months? Did Higgs really think he'd have this bunch whipped into shape that soon? Although maybe it didn't matter to him; he wanted to make a statement, truly believing that somehow an ugly display of domestic terrorism and some serious bloodshed would inspire a revolution. The men who shared his exclusionary, racist, misogynistic views were supposed to join the fight to restore America to some imaginary time when white men ruled, women bowed to their lords and masters, and people of color— if there were any left—served their betters. How a man of his education had come by his beliefs, Spencer hadn't figured out.

"What is it you intend?" she asked, voice clear and strong. She hadn't yet so much as glanced at Spencer or Metz, who stood to one side like soldiers at attention on the parade ground. Pretending they weren't there at all?

"For you?" Higgs asked.

"I mean, your plans. Once you *move*."

If there was irony in her voice, Higgs either didn't acknowledge it or didn't hear it at all.

He launched with enthusiasm into what Spencer hoped would be a short version of his rabid passion.

"What made this country great has been lost since we started paying too much attention to the elites, who believe in opening the floodgates to immigration— and it doesn't matter to them if plenty of those immigrants are the scum of society, criminals who sneaked into the US. What happened to the days when people whose ancestors built this great country decided what direction it would go? Now we have people running for office with such thick accents you can hardly understand them! People that don't look American."

Leah blinked a few times, parted her lips…and then firmly closed them. Definitely not dumb. Then she spoke after all. "That doesn't explain what you plan to do to get attention."

He smiled at her as if she was an acolyte crawling before him. Not that he'd accept her into the fold, her being a member of the weaker sex and all.

"You don't need to worry about the details. Just know it's going to be big. We're going to shake this whole, misguided country and raise an army while we're at it." More prosaically, he added, "You can see why we need to keep our plans quiet until we're ready to launch our op. I'm asking for your cooperation. I don't think I'm being unreasonable. After all, this isn't the worst place to spend the rest of the summer." His sweeping gesture was presumably meant to take in the vast forests, mountains, lakes and wild-flowers. "Got to be one of the most beautiful places in the world."

"I don't suppose you're going to let me go hiking or fishing like I did when I was a kid up here."

"Once you've settled in, why not?" Higgs said expansively. "I think you might learn something while you're here, come around to my way of thinking." He paused, a few lines forming on his brow. A thought had clearly struck him. "What do you do for a living, young lady?"

Please, God, don't let her be an attorney or an activist working with migrant workers or... Spencer sweated, running through the multitude of dangerous possibilities.

"I'm a veterinary technician."

When Higgs looked blank, she elaborated, "I treat injured or sick animals under the direction of a veterinarian. I assist him in surgery, give vaccinations, talk to pet owners."

His eyes narrowed. "So you have some medical knowledge."

"I know quite a bit about health issues affecting dogs and cats, and even horses. Not people."

"Never stitched up a wound?"

She hesitated.

"You might be able to help us. In the meantime—" the colonel pushed back from the table, the bench scraping on the worn wood floor "—I'll have one of these fellows carry your suitcase upstairs for you, and wait while you use the bathroom." He nodded at Spencer.

Was he to guard her overnight? If so, could he let her club him over the head and flee into the night? He'd have to make it look good.

For the first time since she'd come downstairs, Leah looked at him. Her dignity might be intact, but the raw fear in her eyes told him she knew what she faced. He hated knowing she was afraid of *him*.

Earlier, her eyes had been so dilated he hadn't been sure of the color. Had he ever seen eyes of such a clear green? And, damn—the courage she'd shown hit him like a two-by-four. With her fine bones and the red-head's skin that wouldn't stand up to any serious exposure to the sun, not to mention the purple bruising on her puffy cheekbone and beneath her eye, Leah Keaton couldn't hide her vulnerability. It moved and enraged him at the same time.

She was a complication he couldn't afford, but knew he couldn't shrug off, either. Spencer couldn't pretend to understand men like Arne Larson and Ed Higgs who didn't feel even a fraction of the same powerful wave of protectiveness that he did at the sight of her, damaged but using her head and holding herself straight and tall.

He picked up her suitcase and nodded toward the staircase. She rose stiffly and stalked ahead of him as if he was less than nothing to her. He admired her stubborn spirit, but knew it would backfire big time if she tried it on some of the other men. He still couldn't risk offering her a word of advice.

If he had to step forward to save her, it would be only as a last resort.

EVERY NERVE IN Leah's body prickled as she climbed the stairs ahead of Wyatt. She'd felt his gaze resting on her throughout dinner and also while the apparent leader spoke to her afterward, yet his thoughts had remained hidden. It was all she'd been able to do not to shudder when some of the men looked at her. This one almost scared her more because he didn't seem to have a single giveaway. All she knew was that he might be the sexiest man she'd ever seen—and that he had the coldest eyes. Her skin crawled at the idea that he was sizing up her body from his current vantage point. Or was he wishing he didn't have to waste time on the woman who'd stumbled on their training grounds and in doing so became a potentially dangerous problem? One *he* might be assigned to solve?

At the top of the stairs, she hesitated, hoping he'd forget how well she knew the resort.

He said only, "Isn't your room at the end of the hall?"

Her room. Sure.

"We can put the suitcase down and you can get out your toothbrush and toothpaste."

Without looking at him again, she continued down the short hall and went back into the very rustic room that had been designated her cell.

He followed, setting down the small suitcase on the bed, unzipping it and then stepping back. Of course, the contents were in a mess. Thanks to *him*.

Resisting the urge to hide the bra that lay on top, she poked through the tangle of clothing, feeling for her toiletry bag and evaluating what was missing.

Unfortunately, the closest thing to a weapon she'd packed was her fingernail clippers. Useless, but if they were still in the toiletry bag, she'd pocket them.

"Your name is Wyatt?" Appalled, she couldn't believe she'd blurted that out.

His hesitation lasted long enough to suggest he was deciding whether even that much information would be dangerous in her hands. "Spencer Wyatt." His voice was deep, expressionless and tinged with a hint of the South.

Finding the toiletry bag, she asked, "Are you supposed to go into the bathroom with me?"

Something passed through his icy eyes so fast, she couldn't identify it. "I'll wait in the hall."

He let her pass him leaving the room, clearly assuming she knew where the bathroom was. She took pleasure in closing that door in his face.

Honestly, there was enough space in here, he could have come in, too. There were two wood-framed toilet stalls, two shower stalls and two sinks. This bathroom had served for all six guest rooms. It was lucky they'd rarely if ever all been in use at the same time.

The fingernail clippers were there. She hurriedly stuck them in her jeans pocket, brushed her teeth, then used the toilet. Not exactly eager to face him again, Leah thought about dawdling, but couldn't see what that would gain her. Presumably, once he'd escorted her to the bedroom, she'd be left alone anyway. So she walked back out to find Spencer Wyatt lounging against the wall across from the bathroom door.

He looked her over, his icy eyes noting the bag still in her hand, and jerked his head toward the bedroom.

Head high, she obeyed the wordless command, walked into her room and shut the door. Her fingers hovered over the lock, which could probably be picked, and she made the decision not to turn it. Why annoy them?

They'd be annoyed enough in the morning when they discovered she wasn't where they'd left her.

Chapter Three

Lying on the bed in the dark, Leah waited for hours, even though eventually she had to struggle not to fall asleep. Twice she heard men's voices outside her room. The first time Spencer Wyatt's was one of them, the other unfamiliar. She tensed when one of the two walked away. Which man remained? Whoever he was, he didn't even look in.

Sometime later a muffled sound of voices had her hurrying to the door and pressing her ear to the crack in hopes of hearing what they were saying.

"…saving her for himself," growled one man.

The second man said something about orders.

She jumped when a thump came, followed by a scraping sound. Had they brought a chair upstairs so they could guard her comfortably? This had to be a change of shift, she decided.

Damn, she'd counted on one man being stuck on guard all night. He'd get sleepy, nod off, sure he'd wake up if her door opened. But if he stayed alert…

Or, oh, God, was the new guard the one complaining that someone was saving her for themselves? Who was he talking about? The gray-haired leader? Or Spencer Wyatt? What if grumbled defiance led to this latest guard deciding he could walk right into her room, and who was awake to stop him?

Rigid, she wished she'd locked the door after all. At least that would have slowed him down.

Receding footsteps were followed by silence out in the hall.

She needed to get out of here. In one way it might be smarter to pretend to be docile for a few days, until they lowered their guard. But the blatant sexual appraisal from so many of the men scared her more than any thought of being killed. Would she really be safe from rape if she played dumb and stayed?

Leah didn't believe it. At the very least, she could hide temporarily. She wished desperately that she knew what time it was. In her fear, she might have exaggerated the passing of time, until only a couple of hours felt like half the night. She had to go with her instincts.

After slipping out of bed, she put on her athletic shoes and tied the laces while straining to hear the slightest sound. Then she used most of the clothes in her suitcase to create a mound beneath the covers that might fool someone who glanced in to be sure she was really there. Finally, she tiptoed to the closet.

Earlier, she'd pulled the folding doors open. If Wyatt checked on her, she reasoned, he'd assume she was exploring, looking hopelessly for some out. Now, once inside the closet, she gently pulled first one door and then the other closed behind her. Kneeling on the floor facing the right side of the closet, she felt for the crack that betrayed the presence of a removable panel.

Uncle Edward had showed her and her brother the spaces between closets upstairs. She'd have been sunk if they'd locked her in either of the first bedrooms at the top of the stairs. But rooms two and three on each side of the hall had closets with removable panels that *connected* one closet to another. He guessed the builder had intended the few feet to be storage. Guests staying all summer could stow a suitcase away, for example. By the time Uncle Edward bought the resort, though, either the spaces—the passages—had been forgotten, or nobody had thought to tell him about them.

Apparently, all of the interior walls were what he called board and batten, which in the old lodge meant horizontal boards had been nailed up in rows. In the rooms and hall, they'd been covered by either plaster or wallpaper. Nobody had bothered in the closets. If you looked closely, you could see into cracks between the old boards, which might have shrunk over time. The whole subject had come up because her brother Jerry had cackled at the idea of spying on guests in the next room.

After issuing a stern warning against trying any such thing, Uncle Edward had smiled down at his great-niece and great-nephew. "Took me a few years here to notice the outline." He'd looked at the dark, dusty opening with satisfaction. "If we were down South, I'd think these were built to hide runaway slaves. 'Course, this place wasn't built until just over a hundred years ago, long after abolition."

He'd had to explain what abolition was for Jerry's sake. Leah remembered from school.

Now she held her breath, lifted the panel away and leaned it where she'd be able to reach it once she was inside. There hadn't been so much as a creak. If the next bedroom was occupied...she'd have to retreat.

Hesitating, she wished she'd brought a flashlight, instead of intending to rely on her phone. Although, that, too, would have been confiscated. Well, the spooky dark wasn't nearly as frightening as the men holding her captive. And yes, as she started to crawl through the opening and cobwebs brushed her face, she shuddered but kept moving. She could do this. She could deal with a few spiders.

Awkwardly turning around, she closed her fingers around the crude panel and tried to pull it into place. A quiet *clunk* had her freezing in place, but it wasn't followed by anyone swinging open the bedroom door and turning on the overhead light.

Dizzy, probably because her pulse raced, Leah used the short file from her fingernail clippers to pull the panel back toward her until it slotted into place—at least, as well as she could. Sliding her fingers over the edges, she thought it was snug. Her next challenge was to open the panel on the other side while preventing it from falling to the floor. *That* would make enough noise to bring the guard to investigate.

She scooted forward until her head brushed the

rough wood that was the back of the panel leading into the next room.

Somehow, this wasn't nearly as fun as it had been when, as children, she and Jerry used these passages to perplex their parents.

She lifted her hand, feeling for the crack at the top… and something crawled over her hand. Suppressing a shriek she shook off the bug—a spider?—and made herself start again. Finally, she applied a little pressure, then more—and when the panel gave way, she grabbed the top of it.

And then she froze. She reminded herself that one of the men might be *sleeping* in this room. Surely, the group was using at least some of these upstairs guest rooms.

Breathing as slowly and steadily as she could, she told herself she'd made the assumption about empty rooms for a good reason. She hadn't seen anyone go up or come down the staircase, unless it was with her. When the leader had dismissed the group, nobody had headed for the stairs.

Which was reassuring, but hardly conclusive since it had still been early evening when she was escorted to bed.

Would she have heard someone come upstairs, a door opening and closing? Surely, her guard and another man would have exchanged a few words.

Her pulse continued to race and her teeth wanted to chatter. Could she have chosen worse timing for a panic attack? She took a deep breath. She wouldn't hesitate now.

Gradually, a surface level of calm and resolve suppressed the fear.

If she was quiet enough, she could grope around the closet and find out if someone was using it. She could peek into the room without waking a sleeper. If there was one, well, then she'd have a decision to make.

She eased the panel out and leaned it against the back of the closet. Creeping forward, she patted her way along, cursing the complete darkness. She waved her hands over her head, not feeling any hanging clothes.

Would men like this bother hanging up a shirt, or would they just stuff clean laundry into a duffel bag? No shoes, either. But feeling confident the closet was empty didn't mean the room wasn't occupied. Somehow, she suspected these guys hadn't packed big wardrobes for their training session.

If someone really was sleeping in this room, he'd probably set his handgun aside. If she was quiet enough, she could take it. She might actually have a chance then.

If, if, if.

AFTER METZ TOOK his place outside Leah Keaton's door, Spencer had made a point of hanging around downstairs for a while. Higgs wanted to talk through the problem she presented. He rambled, Spencer mostly keeping his mouth shut.

"Would have been better if you'd been able to let her go in the first place," he couldn't resist saying.

The colonel grunted. "That idiot Osenbrock."

Knowing the variety of weapons of mass destruction the group had acquired, Spencer's blood still ran cold. Spencer refrained from saying the whole damn bunch were idiots, including and especially Air Force Colonel Edward Higgs, retired. Spencer could almost wish to be present to see Higgs's face when he learned that he had a snake in his cozy hideaway.

Yeah, not really, Spencer thought, even as he nodded and made supportive noises.

Eventually, he'd had no choice but to announce he was heading for bed. He'd rinsed out his cup and set it on the dish drainer, gone out the front door after a last good-night and headed straight for his cabin. He had no doubt there were eyes on him. At least three of this crowd resented him bitterly. So far, they hadn't risked laying it on the table and thereby earning Higgs's displeasure. Sooner or later, someone would find a good enough excuse to throw down the gauntlet. The longer he could put that challenge off, the more likely he'd get out of here alive.

Although the likelihood of that had plummeted with the arrival of a gutsy woman who didn't deserve to become a victim.

Grimacing, he clumped up on the small front porch of the cabin he'd claimed, unobtrusively drew his weapon and went in for the usual search before he could relax at all.

And before he slipped out again, this time staying unseen, to maintain a long-distance watch over Leah.

THE ROOM PROVED to be vacant, and likely had been for a decade or more. A broken bed frame left the mattress tipping. A front on one of the dresser drawers had split in half.

Light from the hall showed beneath the door.

When Leah tiptoed over to the sash window, she felt a draft. Standing to one side, she felt the cold glass until she found the corner that had broken out.

Taking a chance, she stood right in front of the window, turned the window latch and tried to heave the lower sash upward. Absolutely nothing happened. The warped, painted-too-many-times frame didn't so much as groan. For an instant she thought she saw something—some*one*—move out at the edge of the treeline, but then decided her eyes had tricked her.

She could break out the rest of the glass—but that would alert the guard. If she could swing out, dangle and drop, she might make it to the ground uninjured…but they'd be on her right away. And what if she sprained or broke an ankle? She might not be able to drive, even if the hideout key was still there, and she sure as heck couldn't run away.

If only she knew what time it was. If the door to the hall would crack open without a squeak of rusting hinges.

She stopped herself from creating a list of dire consequences for every decision she made. She'd come this far. She had to peek into the hall and see if there was the slightest chance at all of making it unseen to the stairs. Maybe even whether there were any lights on downstairs, or whether she'd be able to descend into blessed darkness.

No floorboards creaked underfoot as she crossed the room. Prayed the door and frame had been as solidly built. Holding her breath, she very gently turned the knob, then drew the door toward herself a fraction of an inch at a time. It was quiet, so quiet.

Until she heard a muffled sound. A curse?

She had the door open wide enough to allow her to poke her head out into the hall. When she did, she saw a tattooed, muscular guy who hadn't stood out to her if she'd seen him at all. Chair pushed aside, he sat on the floor, leaning back against the door to her original room, legs stretched out. His head sagged to one side, and another snort came from him.

He was snoring. Asleep.

If she'd opened that door, he'd have awakened instantly. As it was…she slipped out into the hall and tiptoed toward the stairs. There was a light on down there somewhere—the kitchen?—but not in the main room.

First step, second, third. She hesitated. One of the stairs had squeaked on her way up. The next— she thought. Gripping the handrail, she stretched to reach the step below, then kept going. Once she was far enough down, she turned her head, searching for movement. For a second guard. For a Rottweiler. For anything, but all remained still.

Within moments she was at the front door.

SPENCER KEPT STARING at the window into the middle bedroom upstairs in the lodge. He'd seen someone; he'd swear he had. Durand, who was currently on guard? Maybe he'd heard something outside, was doing some rounds? But he was an exceptionally big guy, and the figure Spencer had seen had been slight. But how in hell could that woman have gotten past Durand and into a different guest room? He shook his head. Maybe it had been a damn ghost.

He waited. Waited.

Something happened in the deep shadows of the front porch. A person, moving tentatively, emerged into the moonlight and started down the half dozen steps.

Careful, Spencer urged silently. She reached the ground, apparently unheard and unseen except by him, and ran for her car. She went straight for the back fender, crouched out of sight and then stood and rushed around to the driver's side.

A light came on in one of the cabins. For an instant, the woman froze, looking in the same direction.

It was probably just somebody out of bed to take a leak, but you never knew. Spencer had crossed paths with some other night owls from time to time. Paranoia had that effect on a man.

She opened the car door, still unlocked, and jumped in. She was smart enough not to turn on headlights, but seconds later the engine purred to life. Given the silence out here in the forest, it sounded more like a roar.

Lights in other cabins came on.

The car didn't move.

Goddamn. Somebody must have taken the precaution of screwing with her car. Disabled the transmission, maybe, or the CV joint.

Why hadn't Higgs mentioned that to him? Spencer wondered.

Men were running toward her. She flung open her door, fell out and scrambled back to her feet, then took off for the trees.

He couldn't intervene. Even feeling a crack tear open in his iron control, Spencer knew there was too much to lose, and she wasn't going to make it anyway.

It killed him to stay back in the darkness and watch her be tackled by the fastest pursuer. Even down, she screamed and fought furiously. Finally breaking, he started toward them, but too late.

A second guy reached her, and the two of them wrenched her to her feet, still struggling but in an uncoordinated way, as if her limbs no longer worked right.

It was TJ Galt who'd reached her first. Curt Baldwin second. They'd pay for the unnecessary brutality, Spencer swore.

By the time they dragged her to the foot of the lodge steps and dropped her on the ground, the porch light had come on and lights shone in all the cabins. They'd all been awakened and closed in on her. Spencer circled until he could join them in a way that would appear natural.

"What the hell happened?" Spencer asked, just as Higgs pushed his way to the center of the group.

The colonel swore viciously before turning his head. "Where's Durand?"

"Here."

Everyone else drew back from the man who'd failed at his appointed task. Higgs didn't accept failure.

"How did she get by you?"

"She couldn't have." Seeming dazed, Don Durand gazed down at the woman lying in the dirt at his feet. "That bedroom door never opened. Maybe… the window."

All but Spencer looked up at the obviously closed windows.

Was she conscious? It was a minute before he could reassure himself that at least she was breathing. He should have run to her first, pretended to smack her around to avoid this. He gritted his teeth, wishing she'd made it into the woods.

"Get her up!" Higgs snapped.

Galt pulled her up in one vicious motion. One of her eyes was swollen completely shut. The other was open, but dazed. How aware was she?

"Who has a gun?" Higgs demanded.

After a heartbeat, Durand handed over his. Higgs grabbed a handful of her hair and yanked hard while grinding the barrel into her temple.

"How'd you get out?"

It was a long time before she spoke. Then her voice was a mere thread, so faint Spencer found himself leaning forward to hear.

"Way to get from one bedroom closet to another."

Spencer stirred. When he was a kid, his still-intact family had vacationed at a rustic resort on one of

Georgia's barrier islands. He remembered discovering that a panel could be removed in the back of the closet to expose an additional space.

Higgs swore some more. "Why shouldn't I kill you?"

Half the men clustered around her wore avid expressions Spencer had seen too often before, the kind you'd see on faces in the audience at an MMA fight when blood spattered, or in the crowd at a car race after a collision that might leave fatalities. These men were excited, wanted the shock of seeing blood and a young woman go down right in front of them. If Higgs's finger tightened even a fraction…

Spencer pushed forward. "That'd be an awful waste."

"What?" Higgs's head jerked around.

"You heard me." Spencer smiled slightly and leaned on his Southern accent. "She's a real pretty woman."

A chorus of agreement broke out. "Hell, yeah. We can keep her too busy to get in trouble."

Spencer looked into Higgs's eyes. "Give her to me, and I'll guarantee no more trouble from her."

The two men stared at each other; Higgs's eyes narrowed. Spencer didn't dare relax enough even to see how she had reacted, or if she had. Arguments broke out around them. They wanted to share her, or a few of the men thought they were entitled to have her, sure as hell more than that Southern bastard who'd joined the group late. This was a gamble that Higgs would acknowledge him as second in charge by giving him what he wanted.

Higgs's hand holding the gun dropped away, and he used his grip on her hair to twist her toward Spencer. Then he gave her a hard shove, sending her flying into Spencer, who pulled her tight against him.

"She's all yours," Higgs said in a hard voice. "You screw up, on your head be it."

Spencer nodded at their fair leader, then half carried Leah through the crowd, ignoring the chorus of protests and the glares. Every hair on the back of his neck stood up as he broke free and steered her toward the refuge of his cabin.

How the hell *was* he going to control her?

Chapter Four

Supporting most of Leah's weight, Spencer propelled her up the steps to his porch and into his cabin. He laid her down on the futon that would have once served a dual purpose when a family rented this cabin. The damn thing was uncomfortable, but he didn't suppose she'd notice right now. Aware that they'd been watched all the way, he was glad to be able to close and lock the door.

The damage to her face was severe enough this time; he wondered whether her cheekbone might be broken. He worried even more that her brain had been traumatized. Knowing there wasn't a thing he could do if that was so, Spencer gritted his teeth and went to the corner of the room that served as a kitchen. She hadn't moved when he returned with an ice pack and a T-shirt he'd left lying over the back of a chair.

He sat beside her on the futon, wrapped the ice pack in the thin cotton T-shirt and gently laid it over her cheekbone, eye and brow.

She jerked and flailed.

"Hey," he said quietly. "I know this doesn't feel

good, but it's only ice. You've got some major swelling going on."

Her eye—the one that wasn't swollen shut—opened, looking glassy and uncomprehending.

"That SOB clobbered you," Spencer continued, working to keep his voice reassuring instead of enraged. "I'll give you something for the pain once the ice has had a chance to help." And once she demonstrated some coherence. If she didn't…well, that was a bridge he'd cross when he had no other choice.

Her eye closed and a small sigh escaped her.

His hand was cold, but he didn't move it, just kept looking down at her, taking in every detail of her face, from the old and new damage to her lashes and eyebrows, both auburn instead of brown. Just long enough to tuck behind her ears, her hair was ruffled but obviously straight. A high forehead gave her some of that look of innocence and youth he'd first noticed. She had a pretty mouth, now that it wasn't pressed into a tight line.

With a grimace, he corrected himself. What he'd really meant was, *Now that it was lax because she was semiconscious.*

"Leah?"

His anxiety ratcheted up a notch when she didn't respond.

He tried again. "Can you hear me? I need to know how you're doing."

Her lashes fluttered and the single eyelid rose. She tried to focus a still-dazed eye on him. "Why—" she licked her lips "—would you care?"

He'd bent his head closer to hear a question that was more a prolonged breath than words. There were any number of possible responses, but he went with, "You didn't deserve this."

"Tried...run away."

"I know."

"You...missed car key."

Okay, she was with him, if still feeling like crap. He smiled. "I didn't miss the key. I left it for you."

"Car wouldn't drive."

"I didn't do that. Didn't know anyone else had, either."

Tiny lines formed on her forehead above the ice pack. "Why would you want me to get away?"

The side of him that was utterly focused on his mission hadn't. A police response would have majorly screwed up this operation. He'd invested too much in it to want it ended prematurely. But he hadn't been able to stand back and watch her be raped or killed, either.

"I don't hurt women," he finally said.

Was that a snort? He wasn't sure, and she'd closed her eye again.

"If you can hold this in place—" he lifted her hand and laid it over the ice pack "—I'll get you some painkillers."

"'Kay," she murmured.

He kept a sharp eye on her for the short time it took him to dig in his leather duffel bag in the bedroom and return to the main room with a bottle of over-the-counter meds. He had some better stuff tucked away, too, but he'd hold off on that for now.

Bringing a glass of water, too, he helped her half sit up and swallow the pills, then gently laid her back again.

"Have you gotten any sleep tonight?" he asked.

Her nose wrinkled. "Maybe…hour or two?"

That was what he'd thought. "Once the pain lets up a little, I'm hoping you'll be able to get a few hours."

She didn't comment. Spencer had to wonder if her busy little brain wasn't already plotting how to escape. As in, waiting until he had fallen asleep. And, damn it, he did need some sleep. He didn't like his best option here, and she'd like it even less, but he didn't see a workable alternative. Now that he had her safe, he wouldn't let her risk herself unnecessarily…and he was back to focusing first on what he needed to do.

She paid enough attention to him to lift her arms when he asked, and tell him where else she hurt. He manipulated her right shoulder and decided it, too, was inflamed and deeply bruised from when she hit the ground with TJ's weight atop her.

He cracked open another ice pack and applied it to her shoulder. When she started shivering, he grabbed his fleece jacket and spread it over her.

Leah peered suspiciously at him from her one good eye.

Finally, he said, "Okay, tell you what. I'm going to move you to the bed so you can really get some sleep. We'll ice any swelling in the morning." Which wasn't very far away.

She didn't move. Spencer took away the ice packs and tossed them in the small sink. Returning to her, he slid an arm behind her back and said, "Upsy daisy."

"I want to stay here."

"Not happening," he said flatly.

"Why not?"

"You didn't get away. There won't be a second chance."

She twisted out of his grip. "I won't!"

"I didn't ask you." This time he lifted her using both arms.

Her pliancy vanished. She fought like a featherweight champ, landing blows with her small fists. He averted his face and endured as he walked to the bedroom, but when she managed to clip his jaw, he snapped, "That's it," and dropped her on the bed.

Of course she rolled for the other side and thudded off onto her knees, then scrambled to her feet. "If you think I'm getting in that bed with you —"

"I'm not giving you a choice," he said grimly, and pulled a set of handcuffs from his back pocket.

ALREADY SCARED, LEAH completely lost it then. Gripped by a suffocating terror, she knew only that once he clicked those cuffs on her, she'd be utterly helpless.

He was already shifting toward the foot of the bed, expecting her to come around. She threw herself across the bed instead, her shoulder hitting his hard belly when he moved to intercept her. Fighting mindlessly, Leah used every weapon she had, including her teeth and nails. He let out a stream of invectives when she raked her fingernails over his cheek and sank her teeth into his biceps. Sobbing for breath, she kept fighting even as he subdued her with insulting ease, throwing her again onto the bed and, this time, coming down on top of her.

Even that didn't stop her. She bucked and kicked and screamed until he covered her mouth and half her face with a big hand, somehow managing to capture both her wrists with his other hand and plant them above her head.

Now she couldn't breathe at all. With that powerful body, he was crushing her. She wrenched her head side to side until she was able to bite the fleshy part of his hand below his thumb.

"Enough!" he snarled, and before she knew it he'd pushed her to her side and clicked the handcuffs around one wrist. Her face was wet with tears and probably snot as she continued to fight uselessly against his greater strength.

He snapped the other side of the cuffs onto the old iron bedstead and rolled off both her and the bed to land on his feet where he glared down at her, his teeth bared, his hands half curled into fists.

Leah went still, hurting everywhere, terrified in an all new way. She had no doubt at all that he intended to rape her.

I don't hurt women.

Sure. Right. Her shoulder screamed and her head throbbed. One hip hurt, too, and she tasted blood. Her gaze flicked to his powerful biceps where she saw the bite mark. It was *his* blood in her mouth.

"Damn," he said suddenly, and scrubbed one of his hands over his face. When he looked back at her, his expression had changed. Instead of triumph, she thought she saw regret. No, probably pity. But even that was good news, wasn't it? If he felt sorry for her, would a man still rape a woman?

"Let me get a wet cloth to wipe your face," he said unexpectedly, and left the bedroom.

She tugged at the cuffs, just to be sure they really had clicked shut. The metal bit into her wrist. Leah turned her face away from the door.

A moment later she heard his footfall.

"If I sit down, will you attack me again?" he asked in that deep voice tinged with a softening accent.

Did he wear a pistol? She couldn't remember noticing. If she could get her hand on it...

She had to roll her head to see.

No gun.

He held a wet washcloth.

"No," she whispered.

Watching her, those oddly pale eyes unblinking, he sat beside her, much as he had out on the ancient couch. When he'd tried to take care of her, Leah couldn't help remembering.

That didn't mean she was safe from him, though. Why would he have claimed her if he didn't want sex from her?

But she only closed her own eyes when he laid the warm washcloth over her face and very carefully wiped away her tears and probably some blood and, yes, snot. The heat and rough texture felt so good, she heard herself make a tiny sound that might have been a whimper.

"Better?" he asked quietly.

She bobbed her head. Pain stabbed both shoulders, now that her arm on the uninjured side was stretched above her head, but everything was relative.

"Then we need to talk." He paused. "I want you to look at me."

Leah rolled her head enough to be able to see him out of her right eye. The other one had to be swollen completely shut despite the ice this man had applied to it. Why would he have bothered unless...

"You're not going to escape at this point," Spencer said, his gaze steady, his tone rock hard. "You're alive, and not in the hands of one of those animals, because I took responsibility for you. Everyone here will respect that unless they see me as failing. Say, if you make any kind of serious attempt at taking off. It'll be a free-for-all then, and you could end up in anyone's cabin. Or shared between them. Do you understand that?"

After a moment she nodded. She did see that; she just didn't know what kind of threat *he* represented.

"You have to cooperate. For both our sakes, I wish you could stay holed up in this cabin, but that's not an option. I have to participate in training exercises and planning sessions. That would leave you alone. What you need to do is join the other women and imitate them." He paused. "You saw them at dinner."

This time her nod was uncertain. She hadn't paid that much attention. Mostly, she'd hoped for…she didn't know, maybe a signal from one of them? Any hint that one or all of the women would help if they could?

"They're abused women." His expression was grim. "They each try not to meet the eyes of any man but their own husband or boyfriend, and that rarely. They tend to keep their heads down, shoulders hunched. They scuttle across open ground."

Could she act that well? Leah thought so. Fear was a great motivator.

He continued relentlessly. "The women are expected to do all the cooking and cleaning. They don't complain, because they know their role in life. They talk among themselves only when they're working together in the kitchen, and then it's quietly, and about their work. One of the men—the husbands and boyfriends—always keeps an eye on them while they're together. The message is that they can't be trusted."

Feeling growing horror, she whispered, "You'll do that, too?"

"Damn straight I will, as often as I can."

He startled her by planting a hand on each side of her torso and leaning over her. Dominating her, so she couldn't look away from him if she tried. The triple scratches she'd inflicted showed vividly on his angular cheek above dark stubble. A small bump on the bridge of his nose wasn't her fault.

"*I* am your only protection," he continued relentlessly. "You can't forget that. Right now they're all afraid to cross me."

"Even the boss?"

"Colonel Higgs?"

The irony in his voice had her blinking. "That's what he's called?"

"He is a retired US Air Force colonel. He doesn't let anyone forget it."

"That's scary."

His eyebrows twitched. Leah couldn't tell if he agreed or was pleased to have a leader with a legitimate military background.

"I wouldn't say he's afraid of me," Spencer continued. "Wary, maybe. Preferring to keep my loyalty. Apparently, he has no interest in taking you on himself."

She shuddered.

"You might have been safer with him," the big man with the icy eyes told her. "Nobody would have thought to argue with him. I'm…not popular with a few of the men. We may run into trouble if someone works up the guts to challenge me."

We? This bizarre conversation had her bewildered. *Us against them.* Did he imagine she'd be *happy* to be one of those stoop-shouldered, timid, obedient women?

Or… Leah replayed everything he'd said. His expressions, subtle though they were. His actions, if it was true he'd left the hideout key to the car deliberately to give her a chance to get away. His care with her injuries, the flickers of rage she'd seen. Even when she fought, when she hurt him, he'd still been careful not to hurt *her*.

Very slowly, she said, "You're not one of them, are you?"

SPENCER QUIT BREATHING as he stared at her. Only long practice allowed him to keep his face impassive despite his shock. After a moment he said, "That's not a smart thing to suggest. Not to me, and especially not to anyone else."

Her eyes searched his. The impulse to confide in her took him by surprise. Part of it, he understood. Seeing her so terrified of him that she'd fought with crazed ferocity had hit him hard. If she hadn't calmed down, he might have had no choice. As it was…he shouldn't even *think* about trusting her to that extent. One careless word, a reaction that seemed off to one of the men, and he and she both would be dead. She *had* to be seen to be scared of him, unwillingly bowing to necessity, or somebody might get curious. No cover was good enough if someone was willing to dig deep.

No.

Bending even more closely over her, he said softly, "Do you hear me?"

She shrank from him. "Yes."

"Good." He straightened so that he was no longer caging her body with his.

"You can't tell me—" she began.

Spencer almost groaned. She was either very, very

perceptive, or just naturally rebellious. Neither quality served them well right now.

"I've got to get some sleep," he said abruptly, bending to pull off his boots and socks. "I don't think you
have a concussion—your eyes seem pretty focused
to me—but I'll keep a watch for any problems. You
can try to sleep."

Her eyes widened.

Ignoring her, he pulled his belt from the loops, then
unbuttoned and unzipped his cargo pants.

Wearing only the T-shirt and knit boxers, he went
out to the living room to check locks again, pick up
his Sig Sauer and turn off lights. Returning to the bedroom, he briefly thought about switching the cuff from
the bed frame to his wrist but decided against it. She
couldn't go anywhere, and if she attacked him again,
he'd wake up in the blink of an eye and deal with her.
He might have slept on the futon so that she could
relax a little—but he couldn't afford for someone to
look in the uncurtained window above the sink and see
that he was pandering to Leah. Besides—even rocky
ground would be an improvement over the futon.

He adjusted the bedroom curtains to block anyone
trying to steal a look, turned off the light and tugged
the covers out from beneath her so that he could pull
them over both of them. Then he claimed one of the
two nearly flat pillows, doubled it over and stretched
out beside her.

Leah lay rigid, as close to the far edge of the bed as
she could. Given that the bed was only a full size—
his feet hung over at the bottom—that wasn't very far

away. Besides…the mattress was as old as the futon and the stained kitchen sink. Once she nodded off, she'd roll to meet him in the middle.

A rueful smile tugged at his mouth as he pictured how happy she'd be waking up plastered against his body.

Chapter Five

She dreamed about being stretched on a medieval rack. At the same time she was weirdly comfortable, the cozy warmth feeling as if it came from a heated blanket, but more…solid. Comforting.

Leah surfaced slowly, realizing that she lay on her side with her head resting on her upper arm. That arm was stretched above her, and ached fiercely. Not stretched, she thought on a sudden memory; pulled.

And somebody spooned her, his hips pressed to her butt, thighs to the backs of hers. A heavy arm lay over her, his hand tucked—Leah quit breathing. If his hand wasn't so relaxed, it would have enclosed her breast.

His chest felt like a wall. Was it possible she could feel his slow, steady heartbeats?

He. Spencer. The man who'd claimed her and now expected complete obedience as payback. How had she let him wrap her in such an all-encompassing embrace?

When he climbed into bed with her as if that was routine, she'd resolved to stay awake. Obviously, that hadn't gone so well, and no wonder, considering how desperately tired she'd been by then. Not just from lack of sleep. Shock and pain and fear had taken a toll.

Lying completely still, as if she could fend off the reality that she shared the bed with a very large, muscular man who might well have squeezed her breast in his hand while she slept, Leah understood how poorly prepared she'd been for any of this. She'd grown up in a middle-class home with loving parents, had a good relationship with her sometimes irritating little brother, enjoyed college and even her job, although she did want more. Her only major stumble had been being so blind where Stuart was concerned, and compared to her current predicament, that was... normal. Her letting love, or some facsimile thereof, blind her. And to think of the agonies she'd suffered over that jerk. If only she'd known.

Now she had to face the fact that there was a really good chance she'd be gang-raped or—no, make that *and*—killed in the next few days. It would seem her only chance at survival was to obey the stranger who shared this bed.

His pelvis wasn't all that was pressing into her butt, she became gradually aware. That hard bar hadn't been there when she first woke up. His breathing had changed, too.

"I have to use the bathroom," she said loudly.

His chuckle ruffled the tiny hairs on the back of her neck. "Gotcha."

He gently squeezed her breast, gave a regretful sigh, and he rolled away from her. The mattress rebounded without his weight.

"Now, what did I do with that key?" he said.

She growled; he laughed.

A moment later he'd unfastened the cuff on the bed frame. Leah scrambled to get out of bed. She hadn't thought about her bladder until she'd told him that, but now she *really* needed to go.

Amusement on his face, Spencer stepped out of her way. She rushed for the small bathroom. The warped door didn't quite latch, but stayed closed. Relief.

The mirror was spotted, but she inspected her face. It wasn't pretty. She could see out of both eyes, although the one side was still really puffy, the discoloration gaining new glory. The last time she'd had a black eye, a scared Labrador mix had head-butted her in an attempt to escape. This one would be way more spectacular before it was done.

She surveyed the bathroom before she went back out, but didn't see anything useful. A good, old-fashioned straight razor, or even a disposable kind of razor, might have come in handy. But no; a rechargeable shaver lay on the pedestal sink.

Arming herself might be stupid at this point anyway. A razor blade would look wimpy to men all carrying semiautomatic pistols. And really, given her inexperience, even a gun in her hands might get her in more trouble than it would solve.

Whatever else she could say about the man who'd stepped forward on her behalf—an optimistic way of phrasing it—he exuded danger. So much so, none of the other men had been prepared to challenge him, as he put it. That made him the best weapon she could have acquired…assuming he didn't have an end game that had nothing to do with her welfare.

She ran through a plus list. A) he hadn't raped her when he could easily have done so; B) he had done his best not to add to her injuries, even when she was attacking him; and C) he had actually seemed to care that she was hurt and had tried to make sure she was comfortable.

Plenty of negatives came to mind readily, too, starting with the fact that he was a member of a frighteningly well-armed white supremacist militia with big, scary plans. Moving on to B, if she tried something, he could handle her without breaking a sweat; and C, she had no idea how much of what she'd seen was facade and how much real.

She didn't know him, and one of the greatest threats right now was an unreasoning belief that he wasn't a member of the group at all, that he despised them and was really an honorable, good man. Oh, yeah—and she would have been sexually attracted to him in any other circumstances at all.

Maybe even *these* circumstances, which meant… she didn't know. Was this a primitive response to the fact that he claimed to be standing between her and the world?

Not happening, she told herself firmly. She'd do as he asked, for now. What choice did she have? But she'd watch for an opportunity to escape, and she couldn't afford to soften toward Spencer Wyatt—or to entirely trust him.

SPENCER FELT ANTSY from the minute he left Leah in the large kitchen at the lodge and headed out to the shooting range with the others. The women were washing up from breakfast, Lisa Dempsey planning lunch while Jennifer Fuller handed out cleaning assignments. Spencer wasn't sure he could have made himself walk away if TJ Galt had been the one "supervising," but Dirk Ritchie was staying behind this morning. He'd brought the fourth woman along, Helen Slocum.

Helen didn't seem so much terrorized as mentally slow, Spencer had come to think. Dirk could be unexpectedly patient with her, even showing flashes of genuine caring. In fact, he seemed like a decent guy in many ways, which left him the low man on the totem pole in this crowd. Decency registered as weakness here. Spencer made a point of supporting the guy. Dirk's background suggested a reading disability, a lousy school district and a father who was disappointed in his only son's spinelessness. As with Shelley, Spencer wanted to quietly tell Dirk to take Helen and drive away—and not go home to daddy.

He'd as soon not feel sorry for any of this crowd, but couldn't entirely shut down that side of himself.

Obviously, or he'd be able to keep his mind on business. As it was, he should have taken this shot two minutes ago.

He lay prone in the dirt looking through a scope at a target that he'd calculated was five hundred and seventy-five yards out, give or take a little. It was crystal clear. He breathed in, out, in, out…and gently pulled the trigger.

Higgs squatted beside him, peering through military-grade binoculars. "Hell of a shot."

As had been every one he'd taken today.

Higgs was in love with the Barrett M82 rifle, not because of accuracy, although it was fine. What he liked—and why he'd acquired several of these rifles—was that they fired the exact same .50 BMG cartridge used in the heavy machine gun. The heavy-duty round excelled at destroying just about everything up to armored vehicles. Higgs wasn't interested in subtlety. He wanted a big boom.

One of the downsides of this particular rifle was the lack of accuracy for truly long-range shots. In fact, anything over nine hundred yards. Personally, Spencer had preferred the M40A5, one of many descendants of the Remington 700 rifle commonly owned by hunters. He had comfortably made shots at twelve hundred yards and farther, although there were military snipers who could make longer ones. So far, Higgs hadn't asked for anything remotely difficult for a man with Spencer's experience, which meant a simple assassination wasn't on Higgs's agenda.

Now Spencer peeled off his ear protection and rose to his knees still cradling the rifle. "That's it for me. You know I had sniper training at Fort Bennett. I've spent enough time on a range to stay sharp. Let's focus on some of the guys who need the work."

Happy with what he'd seen, Higgs stood, too, letting the binoculars fall to his chest. "I agree. We'll be lucky if any of the men become reliable at even a hundred yards out. We could use another real sharp-shooter, but unless you have a former army buddy you can recruit, we'll have to get by with what we have."

Temptation flickered at the opportunity to bring in another agent, but Spencer was inclined to think the risk was too great. Aside from backup, how much could a newcomer achieve anyway? He was well enough established to be in a good position to be included the next time Colonel Higgs met with his arms dealer. Nailing down who was stealing and selling contraband US Army weaponry to the group was one of his highest priorities, along with finding out the final details of the spectacular attack that Higgs was so convinced would not only deal a major blow to the government, but also fire-start a civil war.

The crack of shots interspersed their few words. Spencer didn't need binoculars to see how badly Tim Fuller, stationed closest to him, was shooting.

Another week or two, he told himself, but he'd thought the same before. Ed Higgs was being cagey even with Spencer, who wanted some serious time alone with Higgs's laptop. As it was, he had to hold out for that upcoming exchange of cash for arms.

He'd had better luck tracing the source of the funding, and managed to share that much with his superior the last time he'd been part of a supply run to Belling-ham and had had a minute to get away to make a call. Some names weren't all, though. A lot of the money was coming from someone who remained cloaked in shadows. Even the one chance to share what he'd learned had been a few weeks ago, but now instead of hoping he'd have the chance again, his gut told him bad things would happen if he left Leah for an entire day.

In fact, when he looked around he didn't see Joe Osenbrock.

"Where's Joe?" he asked sharply.

The older man's gray head turned. "Don't know. Taking a leak?"

The AK-47 Osenbrock had been using lay in the dirt where he'd apparently left it. Spencer had spent time drilling these idiots in how important it was to treat their weapons with care, but nothing he said had sunk in. They thought they were ready, their impatience building almost as fast as their confidence, until they had begun looking at their great leader with doubt. What use was more target shooting? Hand-to-hand combat? Why did they need any of this, when they had the weaponry to shoot planes out of the sky? Spencer had heard the whispers.

Just the other night, for example. Thinking he was alone with Shawn Wycoff walking at the edge of the trees, TJ had said, "I'm starting to think he's all talk." Hidden in the darkness, Spencer hadn't been ten feet away. He didn't miss so much as a mumble. It never occurred to them anybody could be near, far less breathing down their necks.

That arrogance was good. It would bring these fools down.

Unfortunately, it also explained Higgs's continuing hesitation as well as his unwillingness to trust anyone.

Speaking of trust, Spencer said, "I need to go check on Leah. Make sure she's behaving herself and that Joe hasn't forgotten who she belongs to."

Leah's face had looked better this morning, but that wasn't saying much. He still feared she'd suffered a concussion. He'd checked on her a few times in the night and not seen anything too worrisome, but he wanted to be vigilant.

Higgs's eyebrows rose, but he nodded. "I don't need you out here. Let's talk after lunch, though."

Yes. Why don't we talk about who's footing the bills, he thought. *Better yet, some details about your endgame.*

But Spencer only nodded and, carrying his rifle, walked toward the lodge. He was careful to keep his pace unhurried until he was out of sight of the range set up in what had been a beautiful high alpine meadow. They'd undoubtedly destroyed much of the fragile ecosystem.

Then he broke into a run.

LEAH WAS ON her hands and knees scrubbing the floor in the downstairs bathroom when she heard someone stop in the hall. She stiffened, sneaking a look. Without lifting her head, all she knew was that a man stood there, and he wasn't Spencer or Dirk.

Feet in heavy black boots were planted apart, meaning he filled the doorway. Camo cargo pants didn't hide powerful legs.

"May I help you?" she asked timidly.

"You sure can," he said.

Oh, God. She'd heard his name at breakfast. Joe Osenbrock. He hadn't been one of the two who'd tackled her during her escape attempt, but his perpetual sneer didn't make him likeable. Plus, she'd seen hunger in his eyes when he looked at her. Almost as tall as Spencer, he was broad and strong.

Swallowing, she stayed on her knees and kept her head bent.

"See, Wyatt's got no reason to keep you to himself. What he don't know won't hurt him, now, will it?"

She bit her lip so hard she tasted blood. Where was Dirk Ritchie? Had he seen Osenbrock come in?

"You think he won't know?" she asked, still diffident.

"If he finds out, so what? Not like I'd be spoiling the goods." His voice changed, hardened. "On your feet, woman."

Her mind scrambled for any way to get away from this would-be rapist. She couldn't just let this happen. Finally, she straightened her back, lifted her head and met his eyes, holding his gaze. "If you touch me, he'll kill you."

"Nothin' to say I won't kill him, you know."

A dark shape materialized behind him. "*I* say you won't," Spencer said, voice as cold as his eyes.

Joe whirled to face the threat he hadn't anticipated. "What're you talking about?"

Spencer spoke softly, but with a sharp edge. "I'll also tell you right now that if you bother her again, if you lay a finger on her, she's right. I *will* kill you."

"I was just teasing her a little. That's all. Ain't that so, Leah?"

She kept her mouth closed, even though agreeing might lessen the tension that made the air hard to breathe.

Spencer leaned toward the other man until he was right in his face. "Do you hear me?"

"I hear you!" Joe yelled, and stormed forward. His shoulder bashed Spencer's, but he kept going. A slam seconds later was the front door of the lodge.

Spencer took Joe's place in the doorway. "Where's Dirk?"

"I don't know." She used the hem of her T-shirt to wipe her forehead. "He might still be in the kitchen. Why?"

"I expect him to watch out for you when I can't be here."

"I thought he's here to make sure none of us make a run for it."

The grim set of Spencer's mouth didn't ease. "Well, that, too."

"Will you expect TJ Galt to watch out for me? Or Jennifer's husband? Or… Is Lisa married?"

"Not married. She lives with Del Schmidt. And no, I wouldn't ask any of the other men to protect you. Which leaves me with a problem."

How reassuring. "Leaves *you* with a problem? That sounds like *my* problem."

He shot a glance over his shoulder. "Keep your voice down."

Leah opened her mouth again but had the sense

to close it. She hadn't sounded meek or deferential at all, which would set any of the others wondering about him, too.

"I'm sorry," she whispered.

As usual, his expression remained unemotional, even as his gaze never left her face. "Did you have a choice of jobs?" he asked after a minute.

Leah shook her head. "I wouldn't expect to when I'm the newcomer. They don't know me."

"No." He rubbed a hand over his face in what she'd decided was the closest to betraying frustration or indecision that he came. "Finish up here. I'll decide what we're going to do after lunch."

She nodded, hesitated…and went back on her hands and knees to resume scrubbing. Not that this ancient linoleum would ever look clean again.

"I'LL TAKE OVER here this afternoon," Spencer said during a break in conversations around the table while they ate.

Heads turned, the silence prolonged. When Higgs said, "I'll stick around, too," the atmosphere changed.

Many of them had the same interpretation: their leader intended to discuss plans with Spencer, the chosen, while everyone else, the mere grunts, continued physical training.

And yeah, Spencer thought with some irony, he'd been guilty of plenty of apple polishing to achieve just this outcome. What he earned today were some hateful glances directed his way only when the colonel wouldn't see them.

Only Rick Metz kept chewing with no visible reaction. It wouldn't have crossed his mind that he could have a planning role. The question was why Dirk looked relieved. The same man was never allowed to hang around the lodge all day. Spencer wondered if Dirk knew the other women weren't safe from TJ or Tim Fuller.

By God, maybe he should slip Leah a knife so she could protect herself.

Nice thought, but even if she could bring herself to stick it into her attacker, the ultimate outcome wouldn't be good.

Fear of him was her only real protection. He had to say a few quiet words to men besides Joe Osenbrock.

As he and Higgs waited while the other men left the lodge and the women cleared the long table, Spencer tried hard to focus on what might be an important step in closing this damn investigation, instead of on the woman who had become his Achilles' heel.

LEAH WISHED SHE could hear what the two men were talking about at the table, but she couldn't make out a word. She had a feeling it was important, but she couldn't think of an excuse to sidle close enough to eavesdrop. Jennifer Fuller was in the pantry making sure she had everything for tonight's dinner, which was to be lasagna. Leah had noticed that she poked her head out pretty regularly to survey her worker bees. As intimidated as she was around the men, she seemed to relish lording it over the other women.

Helen was well aware of when they were alone.

Now, as she handed over a rinsed pot for Leah to dry, she whispered, "Spencer said something to Dirk that shook him up real bad. Do you know what happened?"

Just as quietly, Leah said, "Joe Osenbrock got me alone when I was cleaning the bathroom and threatened to…you know."

Helen blushed and ducked her head.

"Spencer heard him and was really mad. I guess he thought Dirk should have kept Joe away from me."

"Dirk didn't know nothing about Joe being back here in the lodge. He wouldn't have let anyone hurt you if he'd known!"

Leah hadn't known a whisper could sound indignant. She smiled at the small, anxious woman. "I believe you. He seems nice."

She didn't actually know any such thing, but at least he didn't look at her the way most of the other men did, and she hadn't been able to help noticing that Helen didn't seem afraid of Dirk.

"Spencer was mostly mad at Joe," she confided.

"I bet." Elbow deep in sudsy water, Helen wielded a scrubbing pad with vigor on the pot that had held the baked beans that were part of the lunch menu. They'd been really good, considering the limited resources anyone cooking had to draw on. Plus, the commercial stove and oven had been installed at least thirty years ago. The miracle was that they mostly still worked.

Possibly that was because Uncle Edward had hardly ever used them himself. Most of the time, he'd insisted the hot plate in his apartment was all he needed. Why make baked beans from scratch when you could open a can? Leah remembered her mother's rolled eyes. Mom had bought him a microwave their last summer here, which had intrigued him. It was safe to say that, as her great-uncle got older and crankier, he would have been even less likely to be inclined to bake a cake or cook anything from scratch.

Too bad he hadn't lingered as a ghost. If he could know, he'd be horrified by the consequences of his gift to her. If he'd actually rented the resort to this group in previous summers—and she increasingly doubted that story—he couldn't have known what those men believed, and especially not what they intended. He'd been courtly, old-fashioned in some ways, but also accepting of people's vagaries. Not for a minute would he have condoned hate-mongering or a threat to the country he loved. Having served as a paratrooper in World War II, Uncle Edward had spent time in a Nazi prisoner-of-war camp. Maybe those experiences explained why, upon returning, he'd chosen a solitary life in the midst of one of American's wildest places.

Handing Leah the next pan, Helen whispered again. "Dirk says you *own* this place."

"My great-uncle left it to me in his—"

Helen jabbed her hard in the side. "Sshh!"

"What…?" Oh. Spencer had settled himself in the doorway between the main room and the kitchen, his posture relaxed, his gaze shifting between the two women. Leah almost whispered that Helen didn't need to worry about Spencer—but if his reputation as the baddest man here was to survive, she needed to keep her mouth shut. If Helen told Dirk what she'd said, he could tell anyone.

She was supposed to be afraid of him, and she needed to act the part. In fact, she immediately imitated Helen's fearful posture. But her forehead crinkled as her hand stopped in the act of wiping out the pot. *Wait*, she thought in alarm. *I* am *afraid of him*.

Wasn't she?

Chapter Six

"How would you feel about going for a walk?" Spencer asked once they left the lodge, post Leah's KP duty after dinner. He felt restless, but didn't dare take a run and leave her behind. The sky was still bright, with night not falling at this time of year until close to ten o'clock. Then he took another look at her. She moved without any noticeable pain, but she'd been brought down to the ground hard yesterday. "Scratch that. You're probably beat."

Flashing him a surprised look, Leah said, "Beat? Why…oh. The cleaning. You do know I don't sit behind a desk all day back home, don't you?"

He hadn't thought about it, but of course she wouldn't.

"I'm on my feet all day long. I see patients, package bloodwork to send out or run screens myself. Medicate and give fluids. Assist in surgery. Like just about everyone else, I help clean kennels and runs. And I subdue everything from snarling Dobermans to raging bulls while one of the vets does an exam or procedure. Oh, and then there's the wildlife. We do the care for a local refuge, which means holding down an eagle with a broken wing or a cougar dented by a car bumper. A little house cleaning is nothing."

Spencer would have laughed if he hadn't felt sure they were being watched. He appreciated this woman. Leah's bravado was welcome in place of self-pity.

"Of course," she continued, her tone musing, "on the job I wouldn't be worrying whenever a man walked into the room whether he had in mind raping or murdering me. That does take a toll."

"Yeah," he said, a little hoarsely. "It would do that."

"A walk sounds good. After all," she added wryly, "as Colonel Higgs said, I couldn't be held captive in a more beautiful place on earth."

Spencer turned his head, for a rare moment letting himself take in the extraordinary panorama. It had been many years since he'd spent time in the Pacific Northwest, a fact he suddenly regretted.

White-capped Mount Baker dominated the sky to the southeast, while more jagged, and farther distant, Shuksan would have been impressive enough. Other mountains were visible almost everywhere he looked. This was rugged country, and yet not far from the Puget Sound and Strait of Georgia to the west. They were surrounded by forests that had never been logged, an arc of vivid blue above, thin grasses and a dazzling array of flowers. Once they passed the last cabin, he found himself picking his way more carefully than usual because of the wildflowers.

"This is one of the prettiest times of the year here, with so much in bloom," Leah remarked.

Grimly focused on his task, he'd hardly noticed the flowers until five minutes ago. After a moment he said, "I know a few of these. Who hasn't seen a foxglove or a tiger lily?"

For some reason the idea of him gardening in some distant future crossed his mind. Not like he wanted to spend another decade living this way. Once this was over…what if he bought an actual house? Even thought about a wife, having children. What would it be like, coming home at five most days?

His picture of that kind of life was vague, not quite in focus, but he discovered it did include a bed of flowers and a lawn. He hadn't mowed a lawn since he was a boy.

As if she'd followed his thoughts, Leah looked around almost in bemusement. "My mother is a gardener. I always figured someday I'd have a house and yard, too." She went quiet for a minute, likely reflecting on the very distinct possibility she'd never have that chance. But she forged on. "I remember Uncle Edward telling me about the wildflowers. There." She pointed. "That's an easy one, a red columbine. And yarrow, and bleeding heart, and monkshood."

"Isn't monkshood poisonous?"

"I think so. I don't remember if it's the leaves or the flowers or what." She looked pensive, then shook her head. "Oh, and that's goat's beard and…"

He let the recitation roll over him. He wouldn't remember which flower was which, but he liked that she knew and was willing to talk to him.

"When's the last time you were up here?" he asked at one point.

"I think I was twelve, so it's been forever." A pained expression crossed her face. "I'm thirty-one. I don't know why I never thought to get up here to see Uncle Edward. I loved our visits when I was a kid."

"We tend not to look back." He was ashamed to realize how many friends he'd let go over the years. He couldn't even claim to have a close relationship with his own brother or parents anymore. Disappearing for months at a time wasn't conducive to maintaining ties with other people.

Leah stopped walking feet away from the bank of the lake that filled a bowl probably scoured by a long-ago glacier. That was not where she was looking, though. Instead, she turned a gaze on him that was so penetrating, it was all he could do not to twitch.

Instead, he raised an eyebrow. "See anything interesting?"

"Yes. Is there a single other man up here even remotely interested in the names of wildflowers?"

"It's not the kind of thing we talk about," he admitted, although he knew the answer. No. "Anyway, who said I am?"

She frowned. "Do you have any hobbies?"

He ought to shut her down right now, but she'd taken him by surprise, as she often did.

"I target shoot. That's relaxing." More reluctantly, he said, "When I can, I play in a basketball league." Baseball, too.

"All militant white supremacists?"

"Ah…we don't talk politics." For good reason.

"Why didn't you assault me last night?"

Spencer was offended enough, he was afraid it showed.

"I told you, I don't hurt women," he said shortly. "It doesn't turn me on at all." Except that she had to have felt his morning erection, so she knew that she did turn him on. For all she knew, though, he woke up with one every morning.

She nodded slowly, the green of her eyes enriched by the many shades of green surrounding them. His fingers curled into his palms as he resisted the desire to cup her good cheek, trace her lips with his thumb.

Damn, his heartbeat had picked up.

But she wasn't thinking about him kissing her, because what she said was, "I don't believe you'd blow up innocent people to make a point."

This time he felt more than alarm. "Who says we intend to kill anyone who's innocent?"

"How can you not?" she said simply. "Unless you plan to blow up Congress…"

That idea was enough to make him break out in a cold sweat. He was beginning to fear that Higgs's plans really were that grandiose.

But she shook her head. "I refuse to believe there aren't good politicians."

Having met some decent men and women who had run for office because they believed in service, he conceded her point. "What are you saying?"

"I think you're an undercover federal agent."

He should laugh. Jeer, tell her to take the rose-colored glasses off. He should slap her, which would fit with the role he played.

Instead, he growled, "I told you how dangerous it is to suggest that."

"We're all by ourselves."

She'd made mistakes today. Carried herself with too much pride, looked people in the eye when she shouldn't. Would she be more careful, or less, if she knew the truth?

"If I tell you why I'm here, you have to become an Oscar-worthy actress," he said harshly. "I can't afford for you to get mouthy with anyone, or say something to me when we can be overheard. Do you understand?"

Her expression altered. "Yes. That little episode today with Joe was a good reminder that not only am I in danger every minute, but you are, too."

"I would be either way." He shrugged. "Me demanding an exclusive on you came on top of what some of the men see as Higgs's favoritism. I wasn't popular anyway. Now it's fair to say jealousy and dislike have become hate."

"Isn't hate their reason for existence?" Leah pointed out.

"For the men." Whether the women took the same world view, he had no idea. And it wasn't all of the men. He wished he could figure out how to get Dirk out of the hole he'd dug, but nothing had come to him. There were a couple of others he'd wondered about, but it wasn't his job to separate the deadly fanatics from the ones who were willing to go along. As Leah put it, to blow up innocents.

She didn't say anything else, just waited.

While undercover, Spencer had never, not once, told anyone his true identity or purpose. He'd also never let himself get tangled up with a nice woman who depended on him for her very survival, and who was handling a terrifying experience with dignity and determination.

He sighed, half turning away from her. "You're right. I'm FBI. I've been under with this group for five months now, although we only moved up here for intensive training four weeks ago. Higgs has been on our radar for a long time. Even before he retired, he'd expressed some really marginal ideas. In fact, his obvious contempt for his boss at the time, a two-star general who happened to be black, led to a behind-the-scenes push to early retirement. Unfortunately, it appears that enraged him, helping motivate him to turn militant."

Out of the corner of his eye, he saw that she hadn't done much but blink during this recitation. She'd seen right through him, all right, which made him question how convincing *his* act was.

"I have plenty of evidence to bring down everyone here. We can't let them get to the point of launching their attack. But there's more I need to know. Like when that main event is scheduled for, and what the target is."

"Does that matter if, well, you prevent it from ever happening?"

"Yeah. What if there's another cell training for the same attack? I've seen no indication Higgs is working with anyone else, but we don't have phone service up here. A few times he's made a trip down to Bellingham. Nobody knows what he does while they're shopping for supplies. He could be meeting someone. If he's emailing, it could be from a computer at the library." Frustration added extra grit to his voice. "He has added new posts to a couple of extremist sites, but they're so cryptic we suspect they might really be messages." He gave his head a shake. "We need to keep walking."

"Oh!" She cast a nervous glance back toward the lodge. "Yes, of course."

Circling the lake, he walked fast enough she had to ask him to slow down. He kept talking, telling her his larger goals: making sure they knew who was backing the group, and who was supplying the arms. Moneyed, powerful men were his real target.

"That really is a...a rocket launcher?"

His jaw tightened. "US Military issue. We have two of 'em."

Leah breathed what was probably really a prayer. He agreed with the sentiment wholeheartedly.

Well before they neared the tree line, he said, "I shouldn't have told you this much, but I don't see that it matters. Just remember, even the smallest hint of any of it is a death sentence for me."

She wasn't looking at him. "And me."

"Unless you get the idea you can bargain with Higgs."

Her shoulders stiffened and her chin came up. "I wouldn't!"

"No." He let his tone soften. "I don't think you would."

She sniffed indignantly.

The color of the sky was deepening, the purple tint making it harder for the eye to see outlines.

"This is the end of our discussion," he told her. "I can't be a hundred percent sure the cabin isn't bugged. From here on out, your job is to avoid notice as much as you can."

"What if…if I was able to get a look at Colonel Higgs's room when I'm cleaning?"

"Don't even think about it," he said flatly. "You are not a federal agent. You're a vet tech."

"My life depends on you learning what you have to so we can leave, you know. I'm not going to sit and wait if I can help."

"If you found names or numbers, you wouldn't recognize their meaning. I would. I repeat. The answer is no."

Her chin went back up but she didn't argue again. Spencer wasn't entirely reassured. This was why he shouldn't have told her so much. That said, people talked within earshot of the women as if they were pieces of furniture, much as servants might have been treated in a big house in eighteenth-century England. They could get lucky—but he didn't mention that possibility, because she was too gutsy for her own good. If she got caught where she shouldn't be, *trying* to eavesdrop—she was dead.

They were dead, since he couldn't stand back and let her die, whatever his priorities ought to be.

As they approached the line of cabins, she whispered, "Is Spencer your real name? Or Wyatt?"

Damn her insatiable curiosity.

"It doesn't matter," he snapped.

A faint squeak came to his ears. In response to his irritation, Leah's step hitched and she hunched a little, probably not realizing that she was looking cowed. As little as he liked having that effect on her, her timing was impeccable. That little creep Arne Larson had just stepped out on the porch of his cabin, the one at the end.

"Got her trained, I see," Arne remarked.

Spencer gave her an indifferent glance. "She's smarter than Osenbrock. She knows what's good for her."

Arne laughed, acid in the sound. "Yeah, I heard you told Joe what's what. He didn't like it, you know."

Spencer shrugged. "He's not thinking about what counts. I watched you shooting today and saw a big improvement."

Arne might not like him, but he preened. Spencer's sniper creds inspired some awe among this bunch.

Then he and Leah were past Arne's cabin and the one beyond it, finally reaching his. She trailed him up the porch steps like the obedient little woman she wasn't. She stayed right inside next to the door, too, while he did his usual walk-through with his Sig Sauer in his hand.

THE SHOWER AFFORDED only a tepid stream of water, but it was adequate for Leah to wash her hair. The shampoo dripping down her face stung, though, and had her mumbling, "Ow, ow, ow."

Somebody had absconded with her hair dryer before Spencer grabbed her suitcase. He had even reclaimed her purse, minus everything important.

"I have your wallet," he told her, not offering to return it. "Phone and keys are in our great leader's possession."

She'd heard him use that phrase before, equally laden with sarcasm. Never in anyone else's hearing, of course.

She couldn't wrap her mind around everything he'd told her. He'd confirmed her suspicion and more, but…could he have lied to ensure her cooperation? Of course he could have—but she didn't believe he had. The very fact that he'd gone out on such a limb in the first place for her sake was a strong argument for his honesty and, yes, possession of what some people would call the old-fashioned quality of honor. Personally, Leah was big on honor right now. Where would she be without it?

She towel-dried her hair as well as she could, brushed it and left the bathroom.

Spencer looked up from where he lounged on what she'd realized was a futon in the living area. Every time she saw him, she was hit afresh with awareness of how sexy he was. Partly it was a matter of bone structure and the contrast between icy, pale eyes and deeply tanned skin, but that wasn't all. He had a brooding quality that got to her. And he'd tried to protect her.

He hadn't even taken off his boots, and his gun lay within easy reach. He was prepared for anything at a moment's notice. The tension really wore on her, but he seemed to take it for granted.

"What are you reading?" She nodded at the book.

"Huh?" He seemed to turn his eyes from her. "Oh. It's Calvin Coolidge's autobiography."

"Really? Is he that interesting?"

"You might say he's become relevant again." If there was dryness in his tone, Leah doubted anyone else would have noticed it. "Coolidge endorsed a law in 1924 that cut immigration by half, with national origin quotas. He considered southern and eastern Europeans to be genetically inferior. The law led to something like forty years of reduced immigration. Higgs thought I'd like to read this. I'm not sure he paid any attention to Coolidge's other policies."

"Is it interesting?"

"His prose isn't riveting." With a grimace, Spencer stuck a torn strip of paper between pages as a bookmark. "You ready for bed?"

"I guess."

He ushered her into the bedroom, then returned to the main room to make his rounds of the windows and check locks. For what good they'd do, she couldn't help thinking. There were new, shiny dead bolts on the front and back doors, but two of the windows had cracked panes, and the frames would splinter under one blow. Of course, that would alert him instantly, and she'd already seen how fast he could move.

When he returned, she still stood beside the bed.

He raised his eyebrows.

"You aren't going to put handcuffs on me again, are you?"

"That depends. Can I trust you not to try anything?"

Somebody could be listening, she reminded herself. "I won't." She went for very, very humble. "I know you'll take care of me."

He cracked a smile that made her mouth go dry, so drastically did it alter his face. Not soften it, exactly, but a hint of warmth along with wicked sensuality shifted her perception of him. Sexy when somber, angry or expressionless, he might be irresistible if he just kept smiling at her.

Of course he didn't. Dear Lord, he wouldn't dare get in the habit! Imagine what the others would think if they saw him.

His eyes burned into hers. Had he read her mind? Well, thinking he was sexy, and okay, feeling a yearning ache deep inside didn't mean she was having sex with him.

She managed a glare that resulted in the corners of his mouth curving again, but once she climbed into bed, he did turn off the light before he stripped and slid in beside her.

Even his whisper held a little grit coming out of the darkness. "I'd complain about the mattress, but I like knowing what'll happen the minute you fall asleep."

The trouble was, so did she.

Chapter Seven

Leah had zero chance to get anywhere near her great-uncle's apartment, appropriated by Colonel Higgs. Jennifer Fuller had the privilege of cleaning it, although only when he was there. Otherwise, another of those shiny new dead bolts kept the nosy out.

However tempting an opportunity would be, Leah wouldn't have seized it. Spencer was right; she'd have no idea what she should be looking for. Anyway, she had no desire to find herself in another spot like she had when Joe Osenbrock cornered her. If Spencer hadn't shown up, she wanted to think she could have fought back effectively or that Dirk would have intervened, but she wasn't stupid enough to buy into comforting lies. Joe was muscular, mean and lacking in a conscience. Dirk had an athletic body, but his muscles didn't bulge quite as much, and he struck her as a little quieter and less aggressive than most of the others. Even if he'd tried to step in to protect her—albeit for Spencer's sake, not hers—he'd have had the shit beaten out of him. Then Joe would have been mad.

Today, in between breakfast and lunch, Leah volunteered hastily for cleaning jobs that would keep her in the main spaces and working with at least one of the other women. There were four of them here, instead of five; TJ said Shelley wasn't feeling well.

Lifting benches around the table while Lisa Dempsey swept under them, Leah tried to start a conversation. If she made friends, she might learn something, right? Well, it wouldn't be with Lisa, who completely ignored her, responding only when Leah said something relevant, like, "I see something under there you missed."

She never looked Leah in the eye, either, which was a good reminder to her that she was supposed to imitate the other women, not befriend them.

Jennifer cracked briefly when Leah said, "That lasagna you made was amazing. You must have worked in a restaurant."

"Thank you," she said grudgingly. "I learned from my mother, that's all."

"Oh, well, I hope you have a daughter who'll learn from you."

Jennifer turned her back and walked away.

A few minutes later Helen whispered, "You shouldn't've said that to her. She's had miscarriages. I think—"

A footstep presaging the appearance of Del Schmidt silenced her.

Chagrined, Leah scraped frost out of the old chest freezer. Could Jennifer's body just not hold on to a fetus? One of the veterinarians Leah worked with had had two miscarriages. She and her husband had been devastated.

In this case, though, Leah couldn't help wondering whether abuse from her husband had ended each pregnancy. Maybe that was unjust, but she didn't like the way Tim talked to his wife, or how he'd shoved her hard up against a wall when he thought she was giving him some lip. It was all Leah could do to pretend she hadn't seen what happened.

Spencer was one of the last to show up for lunch, shredded beef tacos and Spanish rice today. He glanced at Leah when she was the last to sidle up to the table and take a seat, but he was immediately distracted by something the man beside him was saying. Shawn somebody. Or was that Brian...Thompson? Townsend? These guys looked an awful lot alike, all Caucasian although tanned, hair shaved or cut very short, big muscles, tattoos on their arms or peeking above their collars. Arne Larson's looked a lot like one arm of a Nazi swastika, which she thought was more than a little ironic, given how the Scandinavian countries had resisted the Nazi invasion. Obviously, he identified with the invaders and maybe even their genocide.

Leah had a sickening thought. What if her mother had married a black or Latino man? Things would have been different if she, a woman with dark skin, had driven up to announce that she owned the resort. Would Spencer have had any chance at all to save her?

No. How could he have? Higgs wouldn't have bothered giving her his impassioned speech about inciting a civil war to restore this great country to the *true* Americans, because she wouldn't have been one in his eyes.

Her appetite scant, she picked at her food and kept her head down by inclination as well as orders, not even looking toward Spencer.

Toward the end of the meal, though, she heard Tim Fuller say into a lull, "We're running low on food. Jennifer made a list."

Higgs mulled that over for a minute before saying, "Wyatt, you take Lisa tomorrow." He scanned the men around the table. "Schmidt, you go, too."

Leah didn't dare look at Spencer to see if he'd betrayed any emotion at all. She hoped she'd succeeded in hiding how she felt, but she was quite sure she wouldn't be able to take another bite, not when she couldn't swallow it. Fear squeezed her throat as if a powerful hand had closed around it.

HIGGS TURNED A cold stare on Spencer, who had stopped in front of him with crossed arms. The two men were on their way toward the obstacle course built their first week up here, taking in part of the meadow and forest. "I don't want to hear it."

Spencer said what he was thinking anyway. "You didn't like me taking Leah out of your control."

Frosting over, the colonel said, "*Nobody* here is out of my control. Did you forget that?"

He had, misjudging how Ed Higgs would see him stepping in to remove Leah from the chessboard. Damn, Spencer thought incredulously, he was going to have to take her and run, tonight while they still had a chance.

"Are you planning to have her yourself?" he asked.

Higgs's eyes narrowed. "I don't rape women."

"You just encourage your followers to do it."

"Is that what you think?"

Jaw jutting out, Spencer couldn't back down. "I think that's what you're threatening. Take me out of the picture, show me how I rate."

"I've developed a lot of respect for you. I thought I could trust you. Since you set eyes on her, I'm having to wonder."

What was it he'd said to Leah? *You have to become an Oscar-worthy actor.* That was it.

He scoffed, "You seriously think I'd let a sexy piece of tail divert me from our plans? I took her because I don't like doing without, and I figured I was entitled. If you want her—" *I'll have to kill you. Nope, shrug as if she's nothing to you.*

Higg's relaxation was subtle. "I don't."

"Then what's the problem?"

"The problem is you getting in my face because I chose you to run an errand and you don't want to do it because you're afraid someone will put a move on her in your absence."

"No," Spencer said coolly. "I'm afraid someone will think they can get away with taking what's mine, and then I'll have to kill him. You don't want to lose a soldier in our war, do you?"

"You said yourself, she doesn't matter worth shit," the colonel said impatiently. "What's your problem?"

"My problem is that I laid my reputation on the line. *That* matters to me. If you expect me to exert any authority over this bunch, it should matter to you, too. If someone hurts her and smirks at me when I get back tomorrow, what's it going to look like if I back down from what I promised?" He let that settle for a minute before shaking his head and raising an eyebrow. "I'm not willing to do that. I'll do your errands tomorrow, but if I find out anyone touched a hair on her head, there'll be violence. I'm just telling you, that's all. Don't be surprised."

Higgs muttered an obscenity. "Fine. I get it. I'll reinforce your message tomorrow. If that'll satisfy you, General?"

Spencer snapped a salute. "It's Captain, as you know quite well."

"I never could verify your service." This was an old complaint.

"The army can be secretive, even with an air force lieutenant colonel. More so when it comes to the records of spec-ops soldiers."

"Especially snipers," Higgs grumbled. "I got nothing out of them at Fort Bennett."

"Well, it's not as if that's something I could fake," Spencer pointed out. "You want to get me a different rifle, I can make a kill shot from over a thousand feet out."

"Why not the rifle you're using?"

Spencer had said this before, but he didn't mind repeating himself. "The M82 loses accuracy over nine hundred yards. It's a mallet, not a stiletto."

"A mallet's what we want, and you're right. You've proved your abilities and more. I'd take one of you over ten of the rest of these grunts."

"They have their uses."

Higgs smiled. "Indeed they do."

Repelled by that smile, Spencer stifled his need to hear Higgs promise that they had a deal. Demanding any such thing would undo all the good he'd just accomplished.

If he had to kill someone tomorrow, he was prepared, but that would do shit for Leah.

His self-control was rarely strained, but as he held back a growl, he was freshly reminded that she'd put more than a few cracks in it.

Scuttling along at Spencer's shoulder in the morning, Leah asked, "Won't Higgs be outside most of the day, like usual?" Spencer hadn't wanted to talk about it last night. In fact, his mood had been foul.

"Probably." His long stride ate up the ground. "He promised to reinforce my message where you're concerned. He knows what will happen if anyone bothers you."

"Well, that's reassuring," she mumbled. Nothing like knowing he'd take revenge for her, even if by then she was a bloody, bruised piece of pulp.

"Stick with the other women and you should be all right," he ordered before they reached the lodge and there was no more chance to talk.

Should was not the most reassuring word in this context.

Since she'd been designated cook for the first time this morning, she had to shove her worries to the back of her mind. With only a little advice on the quantities needed to feed nineteen men and five—no, four—women, she competently turned out pancakes and two platters piled with nice crisp bacon. Nobody said, "Hey, good job," but as they served the food she felt part of the quartet in a way she hadn't before.

Of course they'd pretend not to see if someone like Joe Osenbrock assaulted her in the middle of the kitchen.

During the meal Spencer ate mechanically, never so much as glancing at her. The table was barely cleared when he, Lisa and Del Schmidt went out the door. Feeling hollow, Leah pretended not to notice.

While the other men headed out for whatever training scheduled for today, Tim Fuller took up a position in the kitchen, his irritation plain.

Did he hate this detail? His wife seemed more self-effacing than usual, which made Leah suspect either he'd been posted out of rotation or was missing something especially fun—say, they were going to find out today what happened when they fired a rocket into a big pile of boulders.

Had they tried out their rocket launchers yet? They surely wouldn't dare shoot one upward. Wouldn't that be picked up on air force or civilian airport radars?

As she was setting the table for lunch, two men walked in. Joe Osenbrock and Carson somebody, another look-alike. Joe's expression turned ugly as he looked at her.

"Coffee," he snapped.

She set down the pile of silverware on napkins and wordlessly returned to the kitchen.

"Joe and Carson want coffee," she said.

"I'll pour it," Helen offered.

Leah smiled weakly. "Thanks."

A minute later she set the mugs down in front of the two men, careful to follow Spencer's instructions. Head bowed, shoulders rounded, avoid meeting their eyes. She hoped they couldn't tell that her pulse was racing so fast she felt light-headed.

Neither thanked her, of course. Joe flicked a glance past her, as if checking to see whether anyone was watching.

Knowing she had no choice, she continued setting the table. She finished and headed for the kitchen just as she heard the front door open again, followed by a burst of voices. She hadn't realized Tim had come out to the dining room until she almost bumped into him.

He stopped her with one hand on her arm. "You're a lucky bitch," he murmured. "Don't count on that lasting."

Leah shuddered. The minute he released her, she hurried into the kitchen. Had he been assigned to watch out for her? Was that why he'd followed her from the kitchen...and why Joe had kept his distance?

Maybe...but she knew a threat when she heard one.

GETTING AWAY FROM Schmidt long enough to make a phone call wasn't easy, but Spencer managed. He'd ordered Schmidt to stay with Lisa while he used the john. Then he helped himself to a phone he had spotted at a momentarily empty cashier's station and took it down the hall toward the public restrooms, an office and what appeared to be an employee break room. It was likely password protected, of course, and he had a phone he could use, but he couldn't be a hundred percent sure that it was still secure. Even if it had been found, he doubted anyone in the group was sophisticated enough to know how to record his conversation or trace numbers he called, but better safe than sorry. If he could get away with borrowing—

Yes. He'd gotten lucky.

Thank God Ron answered. "Special Agent Ron Abram."

"This is Wyatt." No, that wasn't his name, but he didn't use his own name even in theoretically safe moments. He had to *think* of himself as Spencer Wyatt. "I've only got a minute."

"I'm glad you called. I've been worrying."

A woman emerged from the restroom, head bent over her own phone as she passed.

"I have problems," Spencer said. He summarized the events of the past few days, from Leah Keaton's arrival to the "deal" he'd made with Ed Higgs to ensure her safety. "Even though I don't want to quit until I have all the info we need, part of me wants to throw her in my SUV and take off. Trouble is, I'm not even betting we'd get away with that. Del Schmidt drove today. I'm wondering if I won't find the starter or alternator have kicked the bucket. Or worse, it runs for five minutes and then dies. As it is, Higgs keeps the keys when we're not using the vehicles."

"You're not driving today?"

"No. I wasn't given the option, which is one reason I suspect sabotage. By standing up for Leah, I awakened suspicion. Higgs has called me on it. I think I talked him around, but I can't be sure."

"If you have to cut and run, we'd have no choice but to raid the resort and pull the plug on the operation."

"Exactly." He watched two teenage boys laughing and bumping shoulders as they headed for the men's room. "Leah's smart. I think she can play her part for a few days. Higgs wants me with him for a meeting Saturday." The day after tomorrow. "I think it'll be a meet to acquire some new arms."

"That's worth holding out for," Abram said.

"I hate keeping a civilian in the mix," Spencer said.

Abram was quiet for a minute. "Damn. I wish you had a panic button."

"You and me both. I can't promise when I'll be able to call again." He saw a woman wearing a checker's nameplate at the cashier station where he'd swiped the phone. "Gotta go."

He quickly deleted a record of his call, shoved the phone in a pocket and strolled that way. Just as he reached it, he said, "Hey! Somebody lost a phone," and bent over, rising with it in his hand.

"Oh, thank goodness!" she exclaimed. "You'd think I'd have heard it drop."

"It's not damaged, is it?"

"Well, there's no crack anyway." She beamed. "Thank you."

"No problem."

When he rejoined Lisa and Del, now heaping packages of meat into one of the two carts, he asked, "We get any desserts? My sweet tooth has been aching."

Lisa almost forgot herself so much as to smile. "I'm supposed to pick up some flats of strawberries and blueberries for pies, and rhubarb for a cake."

"What about some apple pies? Let's get plenty of ice cream."

Nodding in agreement, Del said, "We need to load up on chips, too."

"I'm supposed to keep to a budget," she said nervously.

"If it looks like we're going to run over, I'll pick up the extra," Spencer said. "Remember, we're feeding another mouth, too." Even if Leah hadn't eaten enough to keep a bird alive, as far as he could see. He'd have to get on her about that.

"Thanks," Lisa said shyly. "I don't want to make anyone mad."

"I'll be mad if I don't get an apple pie," Spencer joked.

The mood stayed good as they shopped and then packed huge quantities of food in the rear and on one backseat of the big SUV. Spencer made sure neither of the others saw even a trace of his growing tension as they made the drive heading northeast on increasingly poor roads.

If he found Leah hurt, he wasn't sure he wouldn't

grab the closest fully automatic weapon and start spraying bullets.

When at last they pulled up in front of the lodge, he hopped out, waited for the rear hatch to rise and grabbed bags of potatoes and a couple of flats of canned goods, then took the steps to the porch. He had to shift the load a little to reach the knob, shouldered the door open and walked in. The first person he saw was Joe Osenbrock, sitting beside Tim Fuller at the long table. Spencer clenched his teeth until his back molars hurt.

He passed the two without a word, without pausing long enough to read expressions, and went into the kitchen.

One of the other women was off to his right. He didn't even know which one. All he saw was Leah, turning from the sink, her hands encased in plastic gloves, a scrub brush held in one of them. The relief and something more that suffused her face did a number on him.

"Leah," he said hoarsely.

Can't drop my load and take her into my arms.

He couldn't even ask if she was all right. He hated that.

Her eyes widened at whatever she saw on his face. What she did was flush, draw a deep breath and say, "Oh, good. I was hoping potatoes were on the list. I'm not sure we have enough…" She bit her lip and ducked her head. "I'm sorry."

Sorry for? But he knew. Some men here would have backhanded her for that artless chatter, especially given the implication that he might have screwed up by not buying everything that was needed.

He tore his eyes from her, saw Jennifer watching them. "Where do you want this stuff?" he asked.

"Oh, in the pantry." Maybe reading his expression, she added hastily, "Or…anywhere is good. We can put everything away."

Footsteps behind him heralded Del's arrival with more food. On his heels, Lisa carried more than she should have to.

"Wherever is best," he said shortly, and went to the pantry.

As he made three more trips back and forth from the SUV, he couldn't help wondering what Jennifer thought she'd seen, and whether she talked to her husband. Or whether he listened to her if she did.

After depositing the last load, he said, "I hope dinner isn't far off. I'm starved."

It was Jennifer who answered, the tiniest edge in her voice. "No, not if Leah gets on with that potato salad."

"I'm hurrying," Leah said, sounding chastened.

Turning to stalk out of the kitchen, Spencer knew he'd be happy never to hear her sounding so diminished again.

But if they were going to hold out long enough for him to make this mission a success, that was one wish he wouldn't get.

Chapter Eight

They didn't talk during the walk back to the cabin. With the sun still high in the sky, it might have been midafternoon. Days were noticeably longer here than even in Portland, Oregon, she'd noticed.

Inside, Spencer did his usual walk-through, then said, "Waste of a goddamn day."

"We...we really were running out of food."

He made a rough sound. "Higgs should have sent Ritchie or Jack Jones."

Leah only vaguely knew who the second man was. Would Spencer dare talk like this if there was any chance at all of a listening device?

Maybe. This barely muted contempt went with the arrogance he projected so well. Deliberately, she thought. Higgs would expect it from him.

"I want apple pie tomorrow," he said. "See to it there is some."

Seeing her bristle, he winked.

In her best "I'm nobody important" tone, Leah said, "Jennifer makes up the menu. She doesn't like it when any of the rest of us make a suggestion."

"Tell her it's from me." He flat-out grinned now. "Lisa knows what I want."

Leah rolled her eyes.

Smile gone, he growled, "Did any of the men bother you today?"

"I… No."

His gaze bored into hers. "You're mine. If anyone so much as laid a hand on you…"

"No. I think they're all scared of you."

"They should be."

Neither of them had sat down. It was too early to go to bed. Leah felt restless and could tell he did, too, but they couldn't go for a walk every evening.

Eyes heavy lidded, he took a step toward her, his fingers flexing. The hunger on his face ignited her own. Leah swallowed. Sex was something they could do. In fact, if the cabin was being bugged, they definitely *should* be having sex. And if that wasn't an excuse, she'd never heard one before.

But he seemed to pull down a shutter, turning away from her and saying gruffly, "You have some books in your suitcase. Why don't you get one? I want to read before we go to bed."

Would anybody buy that? But she knew; he didn't really believe there was a bug, he was just being cautious. She should be grateful he wasn't the kind of man who would use "we need to convince any listener" as an excuse to get her naked.

So she only nodded, went to the bedroom and grabbed one of the books at random. She didn't want to read; she wanted to hear whether he'd had a chance to call his office today and, if so, what he'd learned. She wanted to tell him about the threat issued by Tim, and about the inimical way he and Joe Osenbrock had stared at her. She wanted to know what his lips would feel like on hers.

And she wanted desperately to know when he thought they could leave—if there was any way they could without getting killed.

But he'd finally lowered himself to one side of the futon, stacked his booted feet on the scarred coffee table and opened his book. He appeared to immediately immerse himself.

Leah sat at the other end of the futon, which really meant she could have stretched out an arm and touched him, and opened her own book. She read a few pages, realized she hadn't taken in a thing, and turned back to start over. She thought the one side of his mouth she could see curled up. So he wasn't any deeper in the biography than she was in the romance she'd picked up.

The next hour dragged. She read, reread and finally plunked the book down without bothering to save her place. She was going crazy here, and Spencer continued to read as if unaware of her. She felt quite sure that wasn't true.

Her mind wandered.

He hadn't answered her question about his name. She *liked* the name Spencer Wyatt. What if his real name was something like…she entertained herself by coming up with a list of not-so-sexy possibilities. Elmer. Homer. Barney. Cornelius. Wilbur.

All names, she realized, that would have been her grandparents' or even great-grandparents' generation. If she'd been born then and *her* name was Dolly or Kitty or…or Winnie, she'd probably have been fine with Barney.

The name Barney wouldn't reduce the man beside her in any way, she admitted to herself in dismay. She couldn't think of much that would.

I can't fall in love with him, she thought in shock. What a ridiculous idea. This gooey mess of emotions in her were completely natural, considering he'd dedicated himself to saving her life and virtue. And *that* was a silly way to think of a vicious crime like rape.

She sighed. She couldn't exactly whine that she was bored.

Only, she didn't want to know when they'd get there; she wanted to know when they could *leave*.

"Why don't you go take a shower?" he said irritably.

"Fine." Leaving her book where it lay, Leah stomped into the bedroom, grabbed clean clothes and went straight to the bathroom without so much as looking in his direction.

The fixtures were all chipped and stained, but they worked. At least she'd be bored *and* clean.

Or scared for her life and clean.

She was sitting on the toilet to take off her shoes and socks and tug her shirt over her head when the bathroom door opened again, almost bumping her knees in the tight space. Startled, she looked up at Spencer.

He crowded her even more to allow him to shut the door behind himself. Then he squeezed past her and turned on the shower.

"What...?" she whispered.

He crouched in front of her. For a second she fixated on the power of his forearms before being distracted by the long muscles in his thighs outlined with the camouflage fabric pulled tight. Then she lifted her gaze to meet his eyes.

"I thought we should talk," he said in a low voice. "I worried about you all day."

"I really am fine. There was only one weird moment." She told him about Joe and Carson coming in, the glance Joe exchanged with Tim and then what Tim had said.

"That son of a bitch threatened you."

"It wasn't that overt. I mean, he didn't say, 'I'll hurt you.' It was more like, 'Next time I won't stop Joe.'"

"I still want to shove his teeth down his throat." Spencer rolled his shoulders. "Damn. Saturday I'll be gone part of the day again."

A greasy ball lodged in her stomach. "Why?"

"Don't know for sure. Higgs asked me to accompany him for a 'meet.'"

"To buy weapons?"

"That's what I think."

The pale silver of his eyes was almost like glass, except not so transparent. Quartz crystal. Shimmering, clear, but still hiding the secrets inside.

"That was one of your goals, wasn't it?"

"Yeah." He cleared his throat. "But I'm asking a lot of you."

What if she said, *Too much?* Could she persuade him to take her and leave? Leah didn't know for sure, but thought he might choose her if she begged.

It took her only a moment to steady herself. "What you're doing is important. If all goes well, you'll prevent a cataclysmic attack on this country." If her voice shook a little, well, who could blame her? "It's my country, too. What's more, anybody stealing weapons bought with my and every other American's tax dollars needs to be locked up for good."

She'd swear that was pride in his eyes. He lifted a hand to her face, gently cupped the injured cheek and said, "You're an amazing woman, Leah Keaton."

Her tremulous smile probably didn't enhance the kick-butt speech, but it *was* a smile. "And don't I know it."

Now he grinned openly. "Pretty bra, too."

"What?" She looked down at herself and felt her face heat. The vivid green satin probably made her skin look pasty, but she liked the color.

If she wasn't mistaken, his gaze lingered on the swell of her breasts above the fabric, not the bra. He was so close, his hand still holding her jaw, his face nearly level with hers. If she scooted forward...

His pale eyes speared hers. "I won't do that to you." Low, his voice was even grittier than usual.

"Even if I want you to?"

"Even if. You know the balance of power thing. It's swinging heavily in my favor right now."

Leah couldn't deny that was true. But… "I know what I want."

He rose to his feet, letting her see his arousal, but his gaze never left hers. "I want, too," he said quietly. "But we can wait."

She managed a nod, and he left the bathroom.

Did they *have* enough future to allow for some distant, ideal day? she asked herself. But…he was right. Of course he was. What if they triumphed and made it out of here and then she realized she didn't really like him that well? Mightn't she question whether she'd used her body as bribery so he'd keep her at the top of his priority list?

And no, she didn't think he was that man, or she was that woman.

Maybe what she needed to do was believe in him and herself. Believe they'd make it.

She could do that…but she was more aroused than she could ever remember being just from a touch, an exchange of looks.

Now that Spencer knew Leah was willing, he didn't know if he could survive many more nights with full-body contact but him blocked from being able to make a single move. He seriously considered sleeping on the futon, but that would be as torturous in a different way. He still had the original issues, too: he didn't want to be seen sleeping separately from her, and he didn't like the idea of her alone, a room away from him.

Her cheeks were pink when they met in the bedroom, but she wore a long T-shirt over panties that did a number on his libido, slipped into bed and turned her back on him without saying anything.

Spencer swore silently, set his gun within easy reach and stripped down to his own boxers and T-shirt. He turned his back on her, too.

It was not a good night. Far as he could tell, Leah slept better than he did. He couldn't get comfortable, couldn't control his body's reaction to having hers pressed against him, and when he wasn't brooding about why he hadn't taken her up on her offer, he worried about Saturday.

If Tim's suggestion to her meant what Spencer thought it might, she could be in big trouble. Individually, they were all afraid of him, and rightly so. But what if, when he returned, he wouldn't be facing a single man, but several? Would Higgs intervene, or let them tear him up? If he did step in, would the simmer of resentment boil over?

Did Higgs know a couple of the guys were cocky enough to think they could take his place?

Spencer knew he had allies, guys that were glad he could hold the vicious ones in check. Joe Osenbrock, Tim Fuller, TJ Galt and Arne Larson weren't popular with the rank and file. The question was, how many of the others would have the will and guts to stand up with him?

Who should he talk to before he left Saturday with Higgs? Or was there someplace he could stash her before he left? She probably knew this mountainside better than any of them did. She might have an idea.

But then, could he afford the fallout from her temporary disappearance?

Spencer groaned and rolled over again.

One day, a lot of decisions to make—and another night tucked into bed beside Leah.

THE FOLLOWING EVENING, as they left the lodge after dinner, he said curtly, "We're taking a walk." Well aware several men were within earshot, Spencer ignored them. Beside him, Leah ducked her head and nodded.

He strolled down the line of cabins, Leah keeping up. A single sidelong glance let him see her bewilderment.

"What will they think about us doing this?"

He used an obscenity to tell her how little he cared. He *should* care; he and Leah had been so careful to fly under the radar. Somehow, today, he'd met his breaking point.

Leah looked alarmed but was smart enough to say nothing.

When they reached the meadow of wildflowers, he pointed at one with deep pink, almost bell-shaped flowers. "You know that one?"

"Um…a penstemon, I think. There are clumps of hybrid penstemons in my mother's garden."

Last time they were here, he hadn't noticed the faint trace of a path. Left from the days when the resort would have been filled with guests? He followed it toward the lake.

"What did you want to tell me?" Leah asked.

He appreciated her directness.

"I want to talk about tomorrow, but I needed to get away," he admitted.

"Oh. Me, too."

"Everything okay today?"

"Sure. It was a relief having Dirk there again."

"You're getting Del tomorrow. I don't think he'll bother you."

She didn't say anything, but Spencer knew what she was thinking. Would Del stand up to any of the dangerous men on her behalf? Why would he?

Spencer asked himself again if he was doing the right thing. He didn't know any of the potential victims of the planned attack. He knew, liked, admired, wanted Leah. She was the first woman in years who'd gotten to him like this, and he'd only known her for a matter of days. Maybe it was her spirit, relentless in the face of adversity. Or her courage, facing up to dangerous men while suppressing her fears. She'd sure as hell complicated his life. If they had the chance, he could see being happy to have her go right on doing just that.

"Once you sell this place, what'll you do with the money?" he asked, going for the positive. The question was out of the blue, but he was hungry for a few minutes of normalcy. At least, what he vaguely remembered as normalcy.

Obviously surprised, Leah stayed quiet for a minute. Then she said, "I want to go back to school to become a veterinarian. I'd have done that instead of training as a vet tech, except the idea of graduating with such a massive load of debt is really daunting. I'm pretty sure I have the grades and now the experience to be accepted. The money…would make a difference."

"Your parents can't help?"

"I don't want to ask. Mom's a teacher and Dad works for our local utility district. They make a decent living, but they're not rich. They put me through college, and now they should be saving for retirement."

"You intend to specialize as a veterinarian?"

"I don't know. Surgery fascinates me, and I think I'd get bored if I had to do spays and neuters all day, even if they're important." She shrugged. "One step at a time."

Unfortunately, her next step wouldn't be talking to a real estate agent or filling out graduate school applications.

He said gruffly, "I never asked whether you have a boyfriend."

Leah shook her head. "It's been a while. What about you? I suppose it's hard, given your job."

He fixed his gaze on the mountain, gleaming white, somehow pure. "Next to impossible."

"I don't believe that," she said stoutly. When he didn't say more, she asked, "Was becoming an FBI agent always your dream?"

Dream? Spencer wasn't sure he'd ever had one, the way she meant. Given his lousy mood, that struck him as sad.

He didn't love talking about himself, but he owed

her. No, he corrected himself immediately; if he had any thought of pursuing these unexpected feelings for her, he had to open up, at least partway.

"My goal was to get away from home." He hoped she couldn't hear the sadness. "My father and I butted heads for as long as I can remember. I think he loved me—loves me—but his way of showing it was by being a harsh disciplinarian. I joined the army two days after my high school graduation. Barely looked back."

They'd reached the lake now, the surface of the water utterly still, mirroring the rich blue of the sky. Some plants that probably thrived in wetter conditions grew on the shores, but he didn't ask about them.

"I spent ten years in the army." Too much of it killing people. "Got my college degree along the way. A friend who'd left earlier suggested I apply to the FBI, too. I was feeling less sure that the US military was accomplishing anything. I thought I might do more coming at problems from a different direction."

"Isn't one of their biggest divisions counterterrorism?"

"Yeah, I'm in domestic counterterrorism. Unfortunately, we never have the chance to get bored."

"You said you've done this before."

"Gone undercover? Oh, yeah. I'm good at it." His struggles this time all had to do with her.

"I can't imagine living under that kind of stress."

"Right now you are," he pointed out.

She made a face. "That's why I know I wouldn't like it long-term."

"This may be my last time," he heard himself say. "I've almost forgotten who I am."

Ignoring her role, Leah reached for his hand and squeezed.

He turned his body to block anybody watching through binoculars from seeing the physical contact. When she started to withdraw her hand, he held on.

Her cheeks turned pink, but she didn't look away from him. "To me, you're a hero. That's a good place to start."

Spencer shook his head. "Undercover, you get your hands dirty. It's too easy to forget the moral standards you began with. That's one reason—" He broke off. "If I'm ever going to have a life outside the bureau, I figure I ought to get on with it. I'm thirty-seven."

They had reached the edge of the forest on the far side of the lake. His gaze strayed to shadowy coves between tall fir and cedar trees. It wouldn't be such a sin to draw her out of sight and kiss her, would it? If things went south tomorrow... But he refused to think like that. No reason to believe anyone would be stupid enough to attack Leah. He'd made himself clear enough. And what he'd told her last night would hold true until they got free of this bunch. What if she kissed him back mostly because right now she needed him desperately?

Shoring up the walls of his reserve, he released her hand but moved to face her. "Let's talk about tomorrow," he said. "I'd rather you follow your usual routine, but do you know anyplace you could hide if necessary?"

"Now I wish I hadn't given away the hidey-holes between the closets."

He wished she hadn't, either. "No other secret passages in the lodge?"

Leah shook her head. "If I could get as far as the tree line…"

"That would work only if you had a serious head start. Otherwise, they'd be on you like a pack of wolves."

Seeing her already creamy white skin blanch, he was sorry he'd been so blunt, but she needed to know what she faced.

He'd ruled out giving her his backup gun. It would be a disaster if anyone noticed her carrying. He'd also had to consider whether, in a struggle, she could bring herself to pull the trigger quick enough, or at all. However courageous, Leah was at heart a gentle woman, if he was reading her right. Even if she did manage to shoot and kill or at least disable her assailant, then what would happen? He didn't have a suppressor fitted to either of his handguns. The sound of a shot in the vicinity of the lodge versus at the range would bring everyone running.

"Chances are good I'll only be gone for a few hours. Nobody has said anything, so I don't think the rest know Higgs and I are going anywhere tomorrow. I'd try to get you the key to my SUV, but I can't think how to check it out for sabotage without drawing notice."

She was shaking her head even as he spoke. "Even if I could take off…what would happen to you when you get back?"

"That doesn't matter."

Her expression turned mutinous. "I'm not going to just run away and desert you."

"Leah." Unable to help himself, he took her hand again. "If you ever see an opportunity—a good one—take it. Let me worry about myself. You got that?"

She searched his eyes in that way she did, undoubtedly seeing more than he wanted her to. Finally, she said, "I'll think about it."

Always stubborn.

"You do that," he murmured, and turned away to resume their walk.

Chapter Nine

"Turn in here." Higgs leaned forward, the action pulling against his seat belt. "Go around behind the building."

The long, ramshackle log structure along the old highway might once have been a restaurant or tavern. "What's this place?" Spencer asked as he braked and turned into a weedy gravel lot.

"Somebody told me it was a visitor's center back in the fifties or sixties. Then a restaurant and gift shop." The older man shrugged. "Not sure what else. Not a lot of traffic up this way anymore."

The reason this meeting had been set for here.

Given how little traffic he'd seen in miles, he was surprised the highway was maintained this well. About all he'd seen in ten miles or more was beautiful forest, a waterfall plunging off a cliff only feet from the road and moss and ferns everywhere. Pale, lacy lichen draped like tinsel over branches. When they first set off, mist had clung in dips of the road, blurring the outlines of the evergreens. Half an hour ago they'd risen above it.

Spencer tensed as he drove around the building

and saw a pickup already here, parked facing out. It was a dually built for especially heavy loads; black plastic tarps crisscrossed with cord hid whatever was being hauled in the full bed.

"Park so we can load easily," the colonel suggested.

As he backed in, two men climbed out of the pickup, slamming their doors. Even before he saw faces, he noted both men were armed. Of course Spencer was, too, and he felt sure Higgs was, as well.

Turning off the engine and setting the emergency brake, he was slower getting out than Higgs was. He and the older of the two men were already shaking hands when Spencer walked forward.

He knew that face. It set off alarms in him, even if a name to go with it didn't come to him immediately. He just needed to figure out the context where he'd seen the guy before—or his photograph.

Photograph, he decided. In his line of work, he studied thousands. Soon, he'd have a name to go with that face.

The high and tight haircut on the younger man looked military. His scrutiny suggested he, too, was trying to fit Spencer's face into a context. The older guy's was more buzz-cut, graying like Higgs's hair. Same generation, sure as hell their paths had crossed during their military careers. Both, maybe, getting more and more dissatisfied with the direction their country was going as gay marriage became approved, a black man was elected president of the United States and now women wearing hijabs had been elected to congress.

They'd believe passionately that the violent mission they'd chosen was patriotic. Spencer didn't see any hint of deference between them. They saw themselves as equals, he decided. The younger guy was just muscle. Hey, maybe that was all Higgs considerèd Spencer to be, too.

Spencer exchanged nods with both. The closest to an introduction came when Higgs said, "My second-in-command." Two pairs of eyes raked him appraisingly. He lifted his eyebrows but didn't otherwise react.

"Let's get this done," Higgs's buddy said.

Spencer unlocked and opened the rear doors on the Suburban. Evaluating the load, he thought it would fit. Then he joined the younger guy in pulling the cord off so the tarps could be removed.

This was just like Christmas Day, he thought sardonically. What would be inside the wrapping?

THAT MORNING LEAH and the other women hadn't even started clearing the table before Colonel Higgs swung his legs over the bench and said, "I'll be running an errand."

Everyone around the table looked startled, except for Spencer, of course. He nodded. "Shall I drive?"

Higgs took a set of keys from his pocket and tossed them to Spencer. "We'll take my Suburban. It has more hauling capacity."

Spencer gave a clipped nod, took a last swallow of

coffee and rose to leave with Higgs. His gaze passed over Leah without pausing on her, but she made a determined effort to hold on to this last sight of his face as if she'd taken a snapshot.

None of the men moved until they heard the engine start outside. Tim Fuller looked at her.

"Where are they going?"

"I don't know," she said softly. "He doesn't tell me anything."

Every man in the room was staring at her. The effect was unnerving, making it easier to act scared. She stood up and began gathering dirty dishes.

"We're running low on some of the ammunition," one of the men she didn't really know commented.

"He's been promising a new rifle the army is supposed to be testing. I wouldn't mind getting my hands on that." Brian Townsend.

They threw out wilder and wilder ideas. But when somebody said "bomb," a deafening silence ensued. Apparently, there were some things they weren't supposed to talk about in front of the women.

Leah had been pushing through the swinging kitchen door and hoped they all thought she'd already gone back into the kitchen. Carrying a teetering load of dirty plates, Helen was right on her heels. Leah set down her pile, then took some of Helen's.

Jennifer clapped her hands. "Let's hurry! Along with lunch, we should do some baking."

By all means. Bake goodies while the men planned to build bombs.

Not waiting to be assigned a task, Leah filled the

sink with hot, soapy water and began washing while the others brought in the remaining dirty dishes and Lisa carried a coffeepot out to top off mugs.

Leah let most of the talk about the menu go over her head, but when the women turned to discussing what to bake, she decided to volunteer. Staying in the kitchen, in company with other women, would be smart today.

"I make a really good apple-raisin cake." She suggested they think about picking huckleberries, too, currently ripe. "They're as good or better than blueberries, and they'd stretch our supplies."

Picking huckleberries would give her a reason to be well away from the lodge, too. She might be able to give herself a significant—no *serious*—head start. Wasn't that how Spencer had put it? She couldn't help remembering the rest of what he'd said, too.

If you ever see an opportunity—a good one—take it. Let me worry about myself. The ache in her chest told her it wouldn't be that easy.

"I'll ask Tim," Jennifer said briskly.

Leah only nodded. She wasn't sure she'd ever been truly timid a day in her life, and she could only hope all this deference didn't get to be a habit.

Finished with the dishes, she joined the other women in the baking, putting together a double recipe of her apple-raisin cake while they worked on blueberry pies.

After lunch Jennifer reported that Tim said they could maybe pick berries tomorrow, but not today.

Damn.

She assigned Leah to mop the floor in the main room. She was to do beneath the table by hand, Jennifer said firmly.

The scarred fir planks really needed a new finish. After this many years, the original varnish had been almost entirely worn away. Soap and water weren't really good for the wood, she couldn't help thinking, in one of those absurd moments. Because, gee, did it really matter if the floor rotted and collapsed? As things stood—no.

At least the task shouldn't leave her isolated. Helen had to clean the downstairs bathroom today, Lisa to sweep the front and back porches and clean the mudroom. Jennifer intended to reorganize the pantry and continue baking.

The benches pulled out, Leah was underneath the table on her hands and knees when she saw Del go into the kitchen and let the door swing shut behind him. On a sudden chill, she stopped scrubbing. From here, she couldn't hear voices in the kitchen. He'd probably gone out the back to check on Lisa, she realized. He might stay there for a few minutes talking to her. Helen, here in the lodge, wasn't that far away, but more sweet than a lioness at heart.

Leah made herself get back to work. Any minute Del would return as part of his appointed rounds. Anyway, the men were all too scared of Spencer to mess with him. She'd *seen* Joe back down. Still, she listened hard for any sound at all.

Like the sound of the lodge door opening. She

froze. Del might have circled around. That would make sense—

Booted footsteps approached. From her low vantage point, Leah peered out. This wasn't Del, who wore the ubiquitous desert camo today with desert tan boots. This man had on black boots with heavy cleats and forest-green camouflage cargo pants.

Joe Osenbrock.

Staying as utterly still as a mouse that had seen a hawk's shadow nearing, she even held her breath. Did he see her beneath the table?

Who was she kidding? How could he miss her bucket filled with soapy water and probably her lower legs? In fact, he walked right to her.

"Alone at last," he gloated.

Go with ignorance. "Who's there?" She dropped the sponge in the bucket and turned to sit on her butt facing the threat. "Joe? Do you want a cup of coffee?"

"You know what I want."

Maybe she ought to hold to her timid—now terrified—persona, but she couldn't make herself. Still unable to see his face, she said, "Have you forgotten what Spencer said?"

"He's not going to mess with our team. What we're planning is more important than any piece of ass," he scoffed. "He told Higgs that himself." He crouched to look straight at her. "Don't kid yourself that he gives a damn about you."

"I don't." Scared as she was, Leah knew her chin jutted out at a defiant angle. "But I know he *does*

Get Up To 4 Free Books!

Dear Reader,

IT'S A FACT: if you answer 4 quick questions, we'll send you 4 FREE REWARDS from each series you try!

Try **Harlequin® Romantic Suspense** books featuring heart-racing page-turners with unexpected plot twists and irresistible chemistry that will keep you guessing to the very end.

Try **Harlequin Intrigue® Larger-Print** books featuring action-packed stories that will keep you on the edge of your seat. Solve the crime and deliver justice at all costs.

Or **TRY BOTH!**

I'm not kidding you. As a leading publisher of women's fiction, we value your opinions… and your time. That's why we are prepared to reward you handsomely for completing our mini-survey. In fact, we have 4 Free Rewards for you, including 2 free books and 2 free gifts from each series you try!

Thank you for participating in our survey,

Pam Powers

To get your 4 FREE REWARDS:
Complete the survey below and return the insert today to receive up to 4 FREE BOOKS and FREE GIFTS guaranteed!

"4 for 4" MINI-SURVEY

1 Is reading one of your favorite hobbies?
☐ YES ☐ NO

2 Do you prefer to read instead of watch TV?
☐ YES ☐ NO

3 Do you read newspapers and magazines?
☐ YES ☐ NO

4 Do you enjoy trying new book series with FREE BOOKS?
☐ YES ☐ NO

Please send me my Free Rewards, consisting of **2 Free Books from each series I select** and **Free Mystery Gifts**. I understand that I am under no obligation to buy anything, as explained on the back of this card.

☐ Harlequin® Romantic Suspense (240/340 HDL GQ5A)
☐ Harlequin Intrigue® Larger-Print (199/399 HDL GQ5A)
☐ Try Both (240/340 & 199/399 HDL GQ5M)

FIRST NAME	LAST NAME

ADDRESS

APT.#	CITY

STATE/PROV.	ZIP/POSTAL CODE

EMAIL ☐ Please check this box if you would like to receive newsletters and promotional emails from Harlequin Enterprises ULC and its affiliates. You can unsubscribe anytime.

HI/HRS-520-MS20

HARLEQUIN READER SERVICE—Here's how it works:

Accepting your 2 free books and 2 free gifts (gifts valued at approximately $10.00 retail) places you under no obligation to buy anything. You may keep the books and gifts and return the shipping statement marked "cancel." If you do not cancel, approximately one month later we'll send you more books from the series you have chosen, and bill you at our low, subscribers-only discount price. Harlequin® Romantic Suspense books consist of 4 books each month and cost just $4.99 each in the U.S. or $5.74 each in Canada, a savings of at least 13% off the cover price. Harlequin Intrigue® Larger-Print books consist of 6 books each month and cost just $5.99 each for in the U.S. or $6.49 each in Canada, a savings of at least 14% off the cover price. It's quite a bargain! Shipping and handling is just 50¢ per book in the U.S. and $1.25 per book in Canada*. You may return any shipment at our expense and cancel at any time — or you may continue to receive monthly shipments at our low, subscribers-only discount price plus shipping and handling. *Terms and prices subject to change without notice. Prices do not include sales taxes which will be charged (if applicable) based on your state or country of residence. Canadian residents will be charged applicable taxes. Offer not valid in Quebec. Books received may not be as shown. All orders subject to approval. Credit or debit balances in a customer's account(s) may be offset by any other outstanding balance owed by or to the customer. Please allow 3 to 4 weeks for delivery. Offer available while quantities last.

BUSINESS REPLY MAIL
FIRST-CLASS MAIL   PERMIT NO. 717   BUFFALO, NY

POSTAGE WILL BE PAID BY ADDRESSEE

HARLEQUIN READER SERVICE
PO BOX 1341
BUFFALO NY 14240-8571

NO POSTAGE
NECESSARY
IF MAILED
IN THE
UNITED STATES

care about his reputation. You'd be a fool to challenge him."

Seeing the fury on his face, she knew she'd just made a big mistake. *She'd* issued a challenge. To save face, now he almost had to rape her and face down Spencer. What she'd forgotten was that Spencer wasn't the only one to value his tough-as-nails reputation.

Lightning quick, Joe grabbed her ankles and wrenched her toward him. Leah screamed and grabbed for purchase, not finding anything. Her butt slid on the wood floor. No, there was the bucket. Even as he was still dragging her forward, she snatched it up and flung the water, followed by the bucket, too, in his face.

Joe bellowed and momentarily let her go. Maybe the soap stung his eyes. Leah seized the chance to scramble backward, desperate to come out the other side of the table within reach of the kitchen.

Water dripping from his hair and face, he ducked to grab her again. His head clunked against the edge of the table. By now he was yelling a string of invectives.

At that moment the swinging door slapped open and she heard the thud of running footsteps. Whimpering, Leah crawled out from the shelter of the heavy table right beside Del.

He didn't even look at her. His hand rested on the butt of his pistol, though. Beyond him, Jennifer hovered in the doorway, watching.

Joe snarled as he rose to his feet. "Get out of here."

Leah hardly dared take her eyes off Joe, but she turned her head anyway to see Del. What if he shrugged and walked back into the kitchen?

But his hard gaze stayed on Joe and he said, "No. She's Spencer's girl. You got no right."

"He had no right to snatch her away right out from under our noses."

Del's expression didn't change. "You could have done something then. You didn't."

Joe's eyes narrowed to mean slits. "You calling me a coward?" And—oh, God—his hand slid toward the butt of *his* gun.

"That's not what I said."

Preparing to drop to the floor at any sudden movement, Leah hoped Jennifer was smart enough to fade back into the kitchen. Couldn't they feel the tension?

As the two men held a staring contest, she prayed for Spencer to appear. He hadn't expected to be gone long, and it had already been at least four hours.

Joe said in a low growl, "Butt out of this, Schmidt. She's not your business."

"My job today is to watch out for the women. All I'm saying is, you need to take this up with Spencer, not sneak behind his back."

"You and who else will stop me?"

That should have sounded childish, but didn't. The threat of violence had a weight; it raised prickles on the back of her neck. These men wouldn't take a few swings at each other. They'd pull semiautomatic weapons and start shooting. Killing.

Over her.

Would either of them notice if she eased back until she could dart for the kitchen? And would that do any good if Del lost this confrontation?

A man's voice came from the kitchen. Then heavy footsteps. Two men walked in. Jennifer was no longer visible.

Shawn Wycoff, tall, lean and blond, was accompanied by another of the men who'd so far remained anonymous to Leah. He didn't say much around the table, and like too many of the others, was distinguished by a shaved head, a powerful build and full-sleeve tattoos.

When the men took up positions to each side of Del, Leah did edge backward.

The guy she didn't know was the one to say, "What's this about?"

"None of your goddamn business!" Joe snapped. "Get lost."

"He wants Leah," Del said, not taking his eyes off Joe. "I told him to take it up with Spencer, face-to-face, not stab him in the back."

"What's he done to you anyway?" Shawn asked.

"He's suddenly giving us orders? Where was he six months ago? Where'd he come from? Does anybody even *know*?" Joe asked.

No-name said with surprising calm, "I'm betting Colonel Higgs does, or he wouldn't be here. And the only orders he's given are during training. The guy can shoot like no one else I've ever seen, and I had two deployments. I hear while he served he was spec ops. You don't think you can learn from him?"

Joe made a disgusted noise. "He's so sold on himself, I wouldn't be surprised if he didn't make up that shit."

"You think the army would keep a guy who can make his shot from a thousand yards plus as a regular grunt?"

Joe let them know, obscenely, that none of that mattered. Spencer had overstepped himself when he claimed exclusive rights over the only decent-looking woman any of them had seen in six weeks or more.

"Del doesn't have to do without." He was trying for persuasive, which scared Leah enough to have her inching back again.

Should have gone sooner. Should have run for it.

"What say the three of us have a good time? I mean, come on. What's Spencer going to do? Take us all on?" He grinned. "I've seen you looking, Wycoff. You can't tell me you haven't." He tipped his chin at the other man. "You, too, Zeigler."

Zeigler shook his head. "Not me."

"Looking ain't the same thing as taking," Shawn Wycoff told him. His lip curled. "*I* can get women without raping them."

By goading such an unstable man and appearing to enjoy doing so, Shawn might as well have lit the fuse on a stick of dynamite.

Joe's face turned ugly again with a snarl. "You saying I can't?"

"I'm not saying nothing, 'cept Del's right. Take it up with Wyatt. We're teammates. We gotta trust each other. That's the right thing to do."

Hear, hear! Except the idea of Joe Osenbrock "taking it up" with Spencer scared her. He hated Spencer and would kill him in a second, if he could.

Before, he hadn't had the guts to face off with him. After this standoff, with not one but three of the other men looking at him with doubt, he'd think he had no choice.

And, oh, dear God, did she hear a vehicle outside?

FOLLOWING ORDERS, SPENCER drove around behind the lodge to the sturdy outbuilding that served as their armory. It was a natural. Constructed of logs, too, it appeared to have been added some years after the lodge and cabins had been built, which meant it was solid. Even the shake roof was in good shape. Mostly empty when they first opened it up, it had held only a few chainsaws, a heavy-duty weed whacker, assorted hand tools and an old Jeep with a custom-mounted snowplow. A quiet guy named Jason Shedd had given the Jeep a lube job and oil change, replaced a few belts and gotten the thing running. It was too small to be of much use, but Spencer figured you never knew. He'd been thinking a lot about that Jeep in recent days. The key hung on a string from a nail just inside the rusting steel garage-style door.

The trick was that a heavy hasp and padlock on the door ensured it could only be opened by Higgs, a fact that pissed off some of the men. The ones who'd begun to question his leadership.

Spencer really wanted to get his hands on that key.

Now he backed the Suburban up to the outbuilding

door, set the emergency brake and turned off the ignition.

"I'll look inside and see if anyone's there to help us unload," he said, careful to betray none of the edginess he felt.

"Do that." Higgs reached for the door handle.

Spencer crossed the twenty-five yards to the back door into the lodge with long strides. His nerves had been buzzing since they left this morning. Pretending he was unconcerned had taken everything he had. There wouldn't be any relief for him until he saw Leah unhurt, safe.

The unlocked door opened into a mudroom and then the kitchen. Lisa and Jennifer hovered just outside the entry into the pantry, their anxiety palpable.

His heart lurched. Ignoring them, he walked quietly to the swinging door that stood open.

Before he reached it, voices came to him.

"I'll wait." Joe Osenbrock. His voice turned vicious. "But sweetheart, I'll win. I know better than him how to treat a woman."

"Gee, that might be why you're so desperate," Leah said flippantly.

Spencer hoped no one else heard the slight tremor in her voice.

One part of his tension abated. She was still on her feet swinging, which meant she had to be all right.

The ugly epithet from Joe sent Spencer into another state of being, one all too familiar. He felt... very little. Combat ready, he walked into the dining room just as something big crashed.

On the far side of the table, Joe must have just picked up and thrown one of the long benches. He stood above it with his teeth showing, breathing hard, face flushed with rage.

Only a few feet from Spencer, her back to him, Leah faced Joe…as did three men, all in battle stance, hands hovering over their guns.

Voice arctic, Spencer announced his presence. "Seems I missed some excitement."

Chapter Ten

Leah and two of the three men spun to face him. Del Schmidt had the presence of mind to keep his attention on the armed idiot throwing a temper tantrum.

Both gladness and fear shone from Leah. He wanted her to fly into his arms, but at the same time he hoped she'd know better than to do that. They needed to maintain their cover—and he needed to keep his mind on what was coming.

The two men looked relieved at the sight of him. From the sweat and dirt coating them, it appeared Garrett Zeigler and Shawn Wycoff had just come from running the obstacle course.

Harder to tell with Joe. He was either sweat-soaked or had dunked his head under running water.

Spencer nodded at the two backing up Del. He didn't like owing any of this bunch, but this was different. "Thank you."

Garrett Zeigler's lip curled as he glanced over his shoulder. "He thinks he can take you," he said quietly enough not to be heard by Joe.

"He can try." Would he really have to kill Osenbrock? Yeah. Probably. "Higgs and I need help unloading."

Quick as a rattlesnake striking, Joe started to pull his weapon. In the blink of an eye, Spencer had his own in his hand. "I wouldn't mind blowing your head off, and you know I don't miss."

Joe's face went slack with momentary fear, but he blustered, "Hand to hand. Winner takes Leah." His eyes slid to Leah, who looked strong in spirit but physically fragile as she stood with head high and expression defiant.

Not seeing a way out, Spencer inclined his head, even as he held his Sig Sauer in a two-handed stance aimed at Joe Osenbrock's heart. "Tomorrow morning. In the meantime, put that gun down. You've shown us all you're not trustworthy." Seeing such hate in another man's eyes disturbed Spencer, even as he stayed cold inside.

When Joe didn't move, Spencer said, "Del?"

The other man walked around the table. "He's right, Joe. Give it to me. You can have it back later."

That burning stare turned briefly to Del. "I won't forget this."

"Let me have it."

Spencer took a step closer, making sure even Osenbrock couldn't miss his deadly intent.

With a jerky, furious motion, Joe yanked the handgun the rest of the way from the holster and slapped it on Del's outstretched hand. Then he wheeled around and stormed out of the lodge.

There was immediately relaxation in his wake,

although Spencer didn't share it. Joe probably had half a dozen more weapons stockpiled in his cabin. Whether he'd go get one and commit cold-blooded murder in front of his fellow "soldiers" was another matter. This was all about ego, and if he really wanted respect, he had to make the fight seem aboveboard.

Spencer straightened and reholstered his own gun. "Higgs must be wondering where I am. Let's go unload," he said as if nothing had happened.

Leah stood ten feet away, her face parchment-pale, her eyes dilated. Her hands were clenched in small fists. He wanted to know everything that had happened, how it was that not only Del had stepped in, but the other two men, as well. But that had to wait. Right now appearances were everything.

"Don't you have a job to do?" he asked.

Some emotion flew across her face, too fast to read, which was just as well considering they weren't alone. She nodded, but also stole a look toward the front door.

"Del," Spencer said. "Can you stay?"

"That's the plan."

"I need to refill the bucket," she said tightly.

"Throwing it at him was smart," Del said unexpectedly, addressing Spencer rather than her. Still, he'd gained some respect for her, which might or might not be good.

So the bucket hadn't spilled because someone tripped over it. A pail full of soapy water explained Joe's dripping wet hair, and some of his temper, too.

Ignoring all the men, Leah circled around the table

and picked up the bucket, then trailed Spencer, Zeigler and Wycoff into the kitchen. As she went to the sink, the other two women stared at the men.

Walking out the back door and across the bare yard to the Suburban with Zeigler and Wycoff, Spencer asked, "How'd you two get mixed up in that?"

"Del sent Lisa to get help. We were, ah, heading up to the lodge to take a break."

Shawn grinned. "What he means is, the women did some baking this morning. Blueberry pie and an apple-raisin cake. Decided we needed seconds."

"I'll look forward to dessert tonight."

Higgs had the garage door lifted and the back of the Suburban open. "What took so long?" he grumbled.

"Osenbrock was up to the same crap," Spencer said as if unconcerned. "These guys and Schmidt told him he had to take it up with me."

Higgs's attention sharpened. "He attacked Leah?"

"Appears so. She fought back. Del came running. He sent Lisa to get these two."

The colonel flicked a glance at the other two men, then leveled a steady look at Spencer. "Can you handle him?"

"We agreed to hand to hand in the morning." He nodded at the packed rear of the SUV. "Let's get this done. Be careful. Some of the boxes are heavier than they look."

He wasn't sure what was in all the boxes, except the one crate he'd watched Higgs inspect. It held at least a dozen rifles. Markings on some of the boxes indicated they were the property of the US Government. A lot of those contained ammunition to replace what they'd used. Then there was the something mysterious that had had Higgs and his confederate talking quietly for quite a while.

Given half a chance, Spencer intended to find out what other weapon had just been handed to a bunch of alt-right nutjobs.

The men worked in silence, Higgs directing where he wanted each box put.

"Getting crowded in here," Wycoff remarked at one point.

Higgs frowned at the Jeep. "We can move it out of here if we have to."

Spencer liked the idea but didn't want to go on record saying so. Even if the key stayed on the nail inside the armory, he was confident he could hot-wire a vehicle as old as this one. The Jeep was a standard CJ-5, probably dating to the sixties or seventies.

Five minutes later Spencer turned with deliberate incaution and bumped into Zeigler, who bashed a hip into a sharp corner of the old Jeep. Cursing, he barely held on to the box he carried.

"Oh, hell," Spencer said. "I'm sorry."

"Let's get the damn thing out of there." Higgs took care of moving it himself, parking it to one side of the armory. "We can throw a tarp over it if it looks like rain."

"I wonder if you could sell it to some classic car buff?" Wycoff suggested.

Spencer laughed. "I doubt you could give it away. You know how common these were?"

"Yeah." Wycoff studied the rusting metal and tattered remnants of a canvas cover that had snapped on. "It's no beauty, I'll give you that."

They continued to work. Once the Suburban was empty, Spencer moved it to its usual parking spot out front of the lodge and handed the keys to Higgs.

The two men were now alone.

"Osenbrock is becoming a problem," Higgs remarked.

"Becoming? He's an arrogant hothead."

The boss grunted. "I'd boot his ass out, except that would mean turning him loose. Resentment and a big mouth make for a dangerous mix."

"He's a fighter," Spencer said more mildly than he felt. "He believes in our goals."

Higgs's brows climbed. "You plan to leave him alive?"

"Depends how it goes."

"Whatever you have to do." Higgs nodded and walked away.

Spencer followed him only as far as the dining area, where Leah seemed to be finishing up. Sweaty and disheveled, she looked worse than the men who'd come to her rescue—but she was still on her feet, doing what she had to do.

She was also beautiful, even now. In the intervening days, the discoloration and swelling on her face had diminished significantly, making more obvious the delicacy of her features. The pale, strawberry blond hair was sleek enough to fall back in place whatever she put it through.

"Can I get some coffee?" he asked.

He especially liked the glare that should have incinerated him.

She grabbed the bucket and rose to her feet. "Anything else?"

He barely refrained from grinning. "How about a piece of that cake?"

Leah stomped into the kitchen.

It was Helen who delivered the cup of coffee and a generous square of a rich, dark cake. He could see the apples and raisins in it.

"Leah made this," Helen said softly.

"Did she?"

She backed away. "If you need anything else..."

"I'll be fine." He nodded, watching as she hurried away and out of sight. It was unlikely any of the women would go to prison, but he wondered what would happen to her without Dirk.

Shaking the worry off, he took a bite of the cake. The taste lit up all his synapses, as rich as it looked. Sweet, but with enough spice to offer complexity. Damn, Leah could cook, too.

She appeared ten minutes later, hesitating when she saw him but then advancing. "Do you want a refill?" She nodded at his cup.

"Sure. That's fabulous cake. Helen says you made it."

"My grandmother taught me. It's my go-to recipe when I have to contribute to potlucks."

He nodded and lowered his voice. "You're really all right?"

"Yes. He...was dragging me out from beneath the

table when Del came running. He tried to talk Shawn and—"

At her hesitation, Spencer supplied the name. "Garrett."

"Garrett into having some fun with him. He suggested you wouldn't take on all three of them."

Enraged, Spencer ground his molars. "They didn't consider going for it?" If they had…

But she shook her head. "Joe said he'd seen Shawn looking. I had the feeling Shawn doesn't like him."

She was right. With very few exceptions, these were aggressive men, angry at the world. Small as the group was, it had broken into cliques, the alliances shifting.

Leah continued, "He sort of sneered and said *he* could get women without raping them. It was like he wanted Joe to blow."

"Joe's got friends here, but not those three." His voice still sounded guttural. If Joe had had Arne and Chris Binder and TJ Galt backing him, Leah would have been gang-raped. TJ wouldn't have let a marriage certificate stop him.

Slammed by how he'd have felt if he'd gotten back to find Leah huddled in a small, battered ball, forever damaged by that kind of assault, all the violence in his nature rose in outrage. That was a mistake none of them would have survived to regret.

"Are you all right?" Leah still hesitated several feet away.

"Yeah." It was all he could do to clear his throat. "Coffee?"

She took his cup, reappearing a minute later. As she carefully set it down, she asked, "Is anyone else here?"

"No, I think we're alone except for the women."

"Are you really going to have to fight him?"

"Yes."

"He wants to kill you. Did you see the way he looked at you?" She shivered.

"I saw." He reached out and squeezed her hand quickly before releasing it. "He can't take me down."

"You won't underestimate him?"

"No." Hearing the front door open followed by voices, he said, "You'd better get back to work."

Without another word, she fled. Thinking about his last glimpse of her face, Spencer had a bad feeling he'd failed to reassure her. And the truth was, he'd spent most of his time in the military belly down, with an eye to a scope and his finger resting gently on the trigger of a rifle. He'd wrestled and boxed, sure, but had never tried out any martial arts.

He didn't picture Joe Osenbrock embracing martial arts, either, though. They required discipline he lacked. He was a brute force kind of guy. Joe lost it when he got angry enough or things weren't going his way.

Spencer had to count on cold determination defeating blind fury.

LEAH KEPT SNEAKING peeks down the table during dinner. Spencer acted as if nothing at all was wrong. He ignored Joe, but not so obviously that he was doing it as an insult. More as if… Joe just didn't impinge on his awareness at all.

Joe ate, but she doubted he knew what hc was putting in his mouth. He barely took his burning stare from Spencer. Everyone else noticed, which made for awkward conversation and uncomfortable silences.

Shelley Galt had reappeared for the first time in days to help with dinner and join them at the table. Leah could see immediately that she hadn't been sick at all. She'd been beaten. She still moved stiffly, her left wrist was wrapped in an ACE bandage, and while the long-sleeve tee probably hid bruises, the foundation she'd plastered on her face wasn't thick enough to disguise the purple, yellow and black that enveloped her cheek, temple and part of her forehead, wrapping around an eye that wasn't yet quite all the way open.

Leah knew exactly how that felt. Just looking at the other woman made her shake with fury. Once she saw Spencer's gaze rest on Shelley's face. His expression never changed, but she knew what he thought behind the mask.

After dinner the group broke up more slowly than some times. As usual the women took turns refilling coffee cups or bringing second servings of one of the desserts. Helen was the first to be able to leave. Dirk took her hand and led her out the back door. That he didn't mind people seeing him touch Helen, or his tenderness toward her, said a lot about him. Too bad he was part of a group planning some kind of major attack meant to shake the foundations of Americans' faith in their government.

Shelley left alone. TJ had told her to go, she said. No kindness there. Twenty minutes later most of the rest departed en masse, leaving Leah by herself in the kitchen. She peeked out to see Spencer and Colonel Higgs sitting across from each other at the table, engaged in a conversation that even an outsider could see was intense. What were they talking about? The morning fight? Or the attack that was to be the climax of all this planning and training?

She sat on a stool in the kitchen and tried to think about something, anything, except Joe and Spencer slamming their fists into each other, twisting and tangling in combat. Would the other men surround them and cheer on their favorite, like middle-school boys excited by a fight? She shuddered, imagining the rise of bloodlust, and wondered if Joe's death—or Spencer's—would satisfy the audience.

She knew, *knew*, that Spencer would never concede, not with her life at stake. As terrified as she was of being left to Joe Osenbrock's mercy, that wouldn't be the worst part. How could she ever accept Spencer's death?

She couldn't. Wouldn't.

As a woman who cried when an animal hit by a car didn't make it onto the vet's operating table, she wasn't used to wanting to hurt anyone. But there was no doubt in her mind.

If Joe somehow won, she'd make him pay. No matter what it took.

THEY WERE BARELY inside the door of the cabin when Spencer groaned and snatched Leah into his arms. Leaning back against the closed door, he held her tightly, his cheek pressed to the top of her head. This had been one of the most hellish days he could remember.

He should have taken her and fled already, to hell with his job. Yeah, he'd had two breakthroughs today, but the price was too high. He'd been so cocky, too sure he could protect Leah. He still believed he'd come out the winner tomorrow…but what if he didn't? Or what if he won but was injured badly enough that he was unable to keep protecting her? Joe wasn't the only threat.

She burrowed against him. His resistance to making love with her had hit a low. He needed that closeness, that relief, and thought she did, too.

"Leah," he muttered.

She lifted her head from his shoulder, letting him see the tears in her eyes. "I don't want you to do this."

Desperately, he said, "Let's forget it all, just for a while. Can we do that?"

Even with her eyes shimmering wet, he'd swear she saw deep inside him. He made himself wait until she whispered, "Yes. Oh, yes, please."

He tried to start off gently. They'd never kissed before. His good intentions lasted maybe thirty seconds before one of his hands was on her ass, the other gripping her nape. His tongue was in her mouth, her arms locked around his neck, and she seemed to be trying to climb him. He ached to have her cradle his erection. Her taste, her softness, her acceptance and eagerness, her vulnerability and strength, combined to blast his good intentions to smithereens. He wanted to strip her, lift her up against the door and take her without any finesse. He actually started to turn her and gripped the hem of her T-shirt to strip her when he remembered that damn uncovered window.

He couldn't do it like this. A monumental shudder racked his body. The effort of persuading his fingers to release her shirt tore another groan from his chest. Wrenching his mouth from hers, he said rawly, "Bedroom."

Her green eyes were so dazed, he doubted she understood.

Too frantic for her to wait, he bent to slide an arm beneath her knees and swing her off the floor. Since he started kissing her again, he blundered more than walked across the small living room.

As he turned to fit her through the opening into the bedroom, some part of her body thudded into the door frame and she cried, "Ouch." The next second she pressed her lips back to his and the kiss became deep and hungry again.

Once he laid her on the bed and came down on top of her, they slid into the dip at the middle of the mattress. Spencer didn't care. All he could think about was getting her clothes off. As he tugged her shirt over her head and groped for the fastening for her bra, he wished he'd thought to turn on the light so he could see her. Much as he wanted that, he couldn't make himself leave her.

He had to rise to his knees to untie her athletic shoes and peel her jeans and panties down her legs. While he was there, he took care of his own clothes.

He barely had the sanity to remove a condom from his wallet. She was trying to touch him but wouldn't have been able to see well enough to put the damn thing on. He felt clumsy, and realized the dark wasn't responsible. His hands were shaking.

Too much tumult, fierce need and the knowledge that they could fall any minute off the knife-edge that constituted their only safety, all combined to rob him of any patience. The incoherent, needy sounds she was making—moans, whimpers, he didn't know— told him she was as ready as he was.

Sliding inside her was one of the best feelings of his life. Tight, slick, she welcomed him by planting her feet on the mattress and pushing her hips up to meet every thrust. He set an urgent, hard pace that couldn't last. Her spasms, the way she cried out his name, pulled him with her. His throbbing release seemed to last forever. He collapsed, unable to find the immediate strength to roll off her slender body.

For all the joy and satisfaction he felt, Spencer hated that she hadn't cried out his real name. That she didn't even know it. She'd just made love to a man playing a role, not him.

Whoever I am, came the bleak thought.

Chapter Eleven

Leah woke up to find herself alone in bed. She didn't hear a sound. Not the shower or a whistling teakettle or the creak of a floorboard. Where was Spencer?

They'd made love a second time, slower and more tenderly, his voice deep and almost velvety in the darkness, the Southern accent strong as he told her how beautiful she was, how soft. He called her strong, defiant, smart. He hadn't said how he felt about her, but that would have been expecting too much. Really, how could either of them know so quickly?

Just for a minute she pushed back at the sense of dread that would swallow her if she let it, and instead remembered the feel of Spencer's callused fingers, the raw hunger in his kisses, the way he filled her until she felt complete. She wished…she wished so much, but her chest suddenly felt as if a band squeezed, tightening until she couldn't draw a breath.

He wouldn't have left her behind when he went to meet with Joe, would he?

Horrified, she threw back the covers, struggled out

of bed and only grabbed a dirty T-shirt of Spencer's to throw on before she rushed out of the bedroom.

Spencer sat on the futon, feet on the coffee table, appearing his usual composed self. He held a coffee cup in one hand and gazed at her in mild surprise.

She lurched to a stop, her heart hammering. "I thought…"

"I might be gone?" His voice was low and tender despite his impenetrable expression. "I wouldn't do that to you."

"What…what time is it?"

He glanced at the steel watch he wore. "We have twenty minutes."

"I didn't know you'd set a time."

"Higgs did. He wants us to get the fight out of the way before breakfast."

"Oh, God." Her sense of impending disaster wasn't alleviated. "I need to take a shower."

She should have done laundry yesterday at the lodge, she thought in that part of her mind still capable of mundane thoughts. Rooting through her suitcase, she found a pair of jeans that she'd only worn one day and a clean T-shirt. Her last pair of clean panties.

Right now she couldn't care less if she was filthy. Even the shower was only a way to put off facing what was coming.

Clutching the small pile of clothes, she went to the bathroom without looking again at Spencer.

What if…? But she couldn't let herself think that.

She stayed under the thin stream of water only

long enough to get clean before drying herself with the pitiful towel and hurrying to dress. She combed her wet hair, then looked down at herself. Her battle armor didn't seem adequate.

Taking a deep breath, she went back out, set on not letting Spencer see how scared she was. What he needed from her was trust and confidence. She should have felt both wholeheartedly, but the dread remained.

As soon as she appeared, his gaze landed on her. "I've been in fights before," he said calmly.

Some of her fears had to be leaking out, like too-bright light between the slats of blinds. "Don't hold back," she begged him. "He'll do anything to win."

He still looked unfazed. "Cheat, you mean?"

"Yes!"

"Let's go out on the porch."

He rose effortlessly to his feet. Bemused, she followed him. He closed the door behind them and leaned against the porch railing. Leah desperately wanted the chance to soak in the comfort of his strong arms around her, but they could be seen.

Not heard, though, she realized, at least not from a bug inside the cabin.

Confirming her guess, he spoke very quietly. "There's something you need to know. You're imagining that I always take the high road. I don't. I've long since lost count of the number of men I've killed. I told you I was military, but not that I was a sniper. I saw those dying men's faces." Gravel roughened his voice even as he kept it low. "Some of them will haunt me for the rest of my life, but I kept doing what I thought I had to do. If I have to kill Joe Osenbrock today, I won't hesitate. Do you understand?"

"Yes," she whispered. "Maybe I shouldn't be glad, but I am. It's not just for my sake that you need to win, you know."

The bones in his face seemed more prominent than she remembered. "I do know."

She nodded.

"We need to get going."

He touched the back of her hand lightly as they descended the steps. She studied him, bothered by that seemingly unbreakable calm. Today he wore black cargo pants and a gray T-shirt that showed his powerful pecs and biceps, as well as flexible black boots that would allow him to move fast. He wouldn't be able to kick or stomp the way Joe would, but speed was surely more important. At Spencer's belt, he wore his usual black leather holster holding a steel-gray and black handgun. The men here seemed to go armed all the time as a matter of course. Maybe as a law-enforcement officer, Spencer always did. Leah hoped not, that he could sometimes set that part of his nature aside.

The minute they started down the porch steps, she saw the crowd gathered in front of the lodge. Were they excited about the entertainment? Or were some worried about the outcome?

"If you get out of here and I don't," he said in that same low voice, "the attack's set for November 11, Veterans Day. The president is set to speak, although the location hasn't yet been identified. And they have the components to make a dirty bomb. Remember that."

She opened her mouth in an instinctive protest but closed it. Nodded. "Will you tell me your real name?"

He cut a glance at her sidelong. His hesitation was infinitesimal but real, replaced by a flicker of amusement. "Alex Barr. Alex, most of the time. But stick to Spencer."

"Thank you."

That was the last thing she had a chance to say. They'd reached the crowd, now re-forming into a circle. She followed in his wake until she was close enough to the front to be able to see.

Joe Osenbrock already waited in the center. Not patiently; he was pacing, rolling his shoulders, acting like Leah vaguely thought heavyweights did in the ring before the bell.

Spencer stopped to unclip his holster and hand it and the gun to Garrett Zeigler. Then he walked into the clear space within the ring of bodies and stopped, still seemingly relaxed. Despite appearances, he had to be poised to explode into action.

The mood was more subdued than she'd expected. Even low-voiced conversation stopped when the lodge door opened and Colonel Higgs appeared. He walked forward, took in the scene with one sweeping glance, then asked, "Are they both disarmed?"

"Yes." Del Schmidt held up one weapon. Zeigler raised Spencer's.

"Good. Let's not waste too much time with this."

Higgs studied the two men in the ring, his thoughts hidden. Then he said, "Go."

It all happened so fast, Leah wasn't sure which man moved first, only that within seconds they were toe-to-toe, fists swinging. Grunts of exertion and pain rang out. Blood splattered.

Spencer swiped blood from his face with his forearm, then stepped back to let Joe charge past him. When their bodies collided again, they fell hard to the ground. Spencer got a headlock on Joe, but only briefly. They rolled, pummeling each other, grappling for any advantage, punishing each other brutally with fists and holds that contorted their bodies in ways that had her whimpering.

They fought their way back to their feet.

A few men called out. Occasionally a warning, sometimes a "Good one!" But mostly they were silent, so intent on the battle in front of them, she could have plucked a gun from one of their holsters and started spraying bullets.

Except…she couldn't tear her eyes from the savage fight, either.

Twice she had to step back along with the entire side of the circle when the two men flung themselves in that direction. Mostly, she knew she was begging, or even praying.

Please, please, please.

After a strike against his neck, Joe roared with rage and seemed to redouble his attacks. Spencer countered them, once tripping Joe, who crashed to the ground, somersaulted and came back up.

Spencer spat out some blood and jeered at his opponent. "Getting tired?"

With another roar, Joe charged forward like a three-hundred-and-fifty pound linebacker ready to drop the quarterback. But Spencer was not only fast, he was as big a man if not quite so muscle-bound. A quick side step and an elbow to the gut sent Joe to the ground again. He seemed slower to get up, pausing with one knee still down, even his head slightly bent. Was he done?

Spencer came at him with a kick that sent Joe sprawling again, but he latched on to Spencer's leg and brought him down, too. And suddenly, something metal flashed.

"Gun!" somebody yelled, but it wasn't. It was a knife, and he slashed at Spencer. Blood didn't just spatter, it spurted.

Ready to leap forward herself, she saw Spencer grab Joe's wrist and wrench his arm back. Spencer's teeth showed in a snarl; Joe fought that powerful grip in silent agony.

A couple of the men did surge forward, but before they reached the two combatants, Spencer flipped Joe, slammed his hand on the ground to force him to release the knife, and slugged him in the face so hard Joe's head bounced.

The next second he'd gone limp.

Spencer rolled off him and lay on his back, his chest heaving, his clothes blood-soaked.

Above the tumult of other voices, she heard Higgs's. He'd descended into the crowd and now raised his voice. "Wyatt's the winner. Tim, Brian, haul that cheating scum up to one of the bedrooms." He jerked his head to indicate the lodge behind him. "Shawn, Rick, you're responsible for getting Spencer back to his cabin." Higgs looked around, spotting her. "You've had practice sewing up wounds. Make yourself useful."

Oh, God, oh, God. Her teeth wanted to chatter. Somehow, she managed to say, "Do you have a first-aid kit?"

"Townsend, you know where it is."

It took three men to lift Joe and carry him up the porch steps and into the lodge. Leah only peripherally saw them go, Joe's arms flopping. On her knees beside Spencer, she snapped, "I need something to stop the bleeding."

Spencer watched her, one eyelid at half-mast. The socket holding his other eye was grotesquely swollen, purple. His teeth were clenched, and she'd swear what skin she could see was gray beneath the tan. Or maybe it only looked gray as an accent to the shockingly vivid color of the blood.

She bent her head close to his. "You'll be all right. You won."

One side of his mouth lifted as if he was trying to smile but couldn't quite make it work.

Two bare-chested men thrust cotton T-shirts at her. Neither looked very clean, but they were the best she had. She wadded one and pressed it hard against Spencer's thigh, looked around until she saw Del Schmidt and said, "Can you hold this?"

He dropped to his knees and complied. She pulled up Spencer's shirt, used the second T-shirt in her hand to wipe at the blood until she saw a narrow slit over his rib cage, and pressed it down. Panic scratched at her. If there were more wounds, they'd have to wait, but what if one she hadn't found was fatal? The slit frightened her the most. That one was a stab instead of a slice. She hadn't seen it happen. What organs lay beneath?

Out of the corner of her eye she saw someone pick up the huge knife lying in the dirt. Blood dripped from the double-edged blade.

A man ran up carrying a metal box big enough to look as if it held fishing tackle. "Do you want it here?"

"Take it to the cabin," she decided. Three men prepared to lift him, Leah ordering Del to keep the pressure on his thigh while she did the same on his muscular torso.

They moved slowly, awkwardly, with five of them bumping into each other, but finally made it up the two steps onto the porch.

"Not locked," Spencer growled.

The man with an arm under his shoulders—Rick Metz, built like a boulder—fumbled for the knob with one hand and got the door open. Once inside, she said, "Can we pull out the futon?"

Del did it while she used her free hand to maintain pressure on Spencer's thigh, too. The mattress looked grungy enough she wished desperately for a clean sheet to lay over it, but hadn't seen one. Pain tightened Spencer's face until it was all bones and skin stretched taut between them. He groaned when they laid him down.

To her distant surprise, the men continued to follow her orders. One put on water to boil on the single working burner here, while another ran for the lodge to boil more. A third went for any clean bedding and towels he could find.

Spencer never looked away from her.

HE COULDN'T DIE.

Through the pain, that was all Spencer could think. Leah needed him. *Don't give in. Don't lose consciousness.*

A couple of times she whispered, "Stay with me," and once he even managed a nod. He didn't know if she meant stay in the sense that he had to remain conscious, or that he couldn't abandon her by dying. Either way, he hung on. At least he was done with Joe, who was as good as a dead man.

The guys around him seemed to be doing their best for him. He wasn't even sure who *was* here. He'd have had to look away from Leah to be sure, and he couldn't do that.

He managed to tell her he had pills in his duffel. At least, he thought he'd told her.

Don't give in. God, that hurts. He wanted to curl up to protect his belly, sensing that wound was the most dangerous. If the knife had sliced into his guts, all the resolve in the world wouldn't save him. Half-digested food would be spilling into the abdominal cavity, introducing bacteria where it didn't belong.

But Leah looked focused and determined in a way he didn't remember seeing her before. She was fighting for him, and he could do his part.

Don't give in. Trust her.

He floated in a sea of pain as she worked. There had to be broken bones.

Paper ripped. Somehow, she'd come to have a wicked-looking pair of scissors in her hand and was cutting most of his clothes off him. Wet washcloths, hot enough to have him jerking involuntarily, ran over his legs.

"I'll need to stitch that one up," he heard her say to someone else.

All he felt was pressure on his thigh again.

Once, they rolled him. His back hurt like hell, but in a generalized way.

"Man, he's going to be one solid bruise," a familiar voice said. Del.

It went on like that. He hazily understood that they were searching his body for knife wounds.

"Think the blade hit a rib," Leah said. "If it went very deep…"

He lost the thread of what she was saying.

Eventually, something cold was sprayed on his thigh. Her face appeared above his. "This should numb you enough to help," she said.

Still gritting his teeth, he nodded.

He felt the needle pricking in and out of his flesh. Pricking, hell; stabbing. The spray hadn't numbed anything, but he fought to hold still.

Then on his torso, almost on his side. He couldn't stop a raw sound from escaping.

They produced ice and what he vaguely saw were bags of frozen vegetables to lay on his face and half a dozen other places on his body. The worst bruising? He didn't know, only that the cold burned.

Time passed. He wasn't always sure he *was* conscious. Leah was his anchor, distressing him when she moved out of his line of sight a few times. Dripping ice packs and frozen veggies were removed and replaced at least once.

Rick—yes, that was Rick Metz—was the first to leave and not reappear. Given his lack of emotional content, Rick was a strange one to tend him with care.

When Spencer was able to roll his head slightly, he saw Shawn Wycoff and Del Schmidt. They were more logical as nursemaids. He also became aware that when Leah asked for something, they jumped. Funny that Higgs had appointed her medical director early on. The first day? He didn't remember. Spencer hadn't guessed *he* would be the one to need whatever trauma-care expertise she possessed.

He had to get her to safety so that she could go to veterinary school, the way she deserved. Since the slightest move brought stabbing pains—yeah, that was a pun—he couldn't figure out how he'd protect her, but he'd do it. Somehow.

He surfaced to hear her thanking the two men, sounding almost tearful. Del shrugged. "Let us know what you need."

Say, *I need to go home. Help me get away.*

Of course she didn't. "I will."

The door closed quietly behind them. The mattress shifted enough that he knew Leah had sat down beside him. Her fingertips stroking his forehead was the first good thing he'd felt.

No, he could wriggle his toes with no pain. In fact, thanks to his boots, his feet seemed unscathed. That was good news. If they had to walk out of here, that was what they'd do, he decided.

"You with me?" she asked softly, her eyes so vividly green he would have been happy never to look away.

"Yah," he mumbled.

Her smile lit the room like the sun coming out from behind a cloud. She sobered faster than he liked.

"Thank heavens you didn't lose consciousness! Even so, I'd give a lot to be able to send you for X-rays, or even a CT scan. I think your left wrist might be broken, although I can't be sure. It's wrapped tight enough to immobilize it."

He arrowed in on his wrist. Yeah, that felt like a break. Ribs, too, he guessed, although those might be only cracks or even just bruising.

He could hope.

"It's really lucky you had that oxycodone. Aspirin wouldn't have helped much." She gave an exaggerated shudder.

He shared that gratitude. So he had told her. He hadn't quite realized what those pills he'd swallowed were.

"What will they do with Joe?" she asked, worry

carving lines in her forehead. "Should I go volunteer to look at him?"

"No." That sounded almost normal. "Don't shink—" he tried harder "—*think* he'll survive."

"Why? Did you—" Comprehension changed her face. "You mean…"

He managed a tiny nod. Best not to say it out loud.

"Oh, dear God," Leah whispered.

He somehow lifted a hand enough to lay it on her arm. She looked down, then up to meet his eyes, and understood. *Careful.*

"Later I'll have Del and Shawn or somebody else move you to the bedroom. I know the futon must be horribly uncomfortable. But if we were going to ruin one or the other with blood, I decided it should be the futon."

He absolutely agreed. After last night, he'd developed fond feelings for that bed.

"*Could* somebody take you to an ER?"

She meant, would it be allowed. "No," he said. Steeled himself and added, "Okay."

That earned him a wrinkled nose. "You're a long way from *okay*. But I suppose you must have been injured during your years in the military."

Another slight inclination of his head, although even that set off fireworks. He had to close his eyes momentarily.

Yes, he'd been hospitalized several times. Strange to think that he might have come closer to dying today than he had from bullet wounds or shrapnel from an IED. If that knife blade had plunged deeper, or struck higher or lower, it could easily have been curtains for him, given that the best medical care available was from a veterinary technician with access only to a basic first-aid kit. He'd been damned lucky, and he wouldn't waste that luck.

He really was done with undercover gigs. No hostage rescue for him, either. He'd transfer as soon as he could—once he'd taken down Colonel Higgs and his hatefully misguided army.

And Leah. If she wanted him, he'd do what he had to do to have her in his life, too. He could transfer to the Seattle office, or the office closest to wherever she would be attending grad school.

All good plans. Unfortunately, right this minute a soon-to-be-needed trip to the bathroom reared ahead like Kilimanjaro. Only positive was, he knew he was thinking more clearly.

These injuries would buy him a day or two off from a role that he hadn't been able to set down in months. That said, would Leah still be expected to cook and clean rather than care for him? That would leave her vulnerable…although he thought Higgs had been pissed off enough about Joe's behavior to lay down the law where she was concerned.

Maybe.

Spencer grunted. What he needed was to get back on his feet as quickly as possible. For starters, he wouldn't have a chance to pocket the key to start the Jeep unless he rejoined activities, even if only as a spectator.

A good place to start was with that short journey

to the bathroom. The hell he was going to piss in a jar and make Leah dump it out.

Despite the explosion of pain, he started to shift his body toward the edge of the futon amid her cries of, "What are you *doing*? Stop!"

Chapter Twelve

The stubborn man insisted she lay a sheet over the dirty, blood-stained futon mattress and bring him some pillows so he could spend the day out there. Leah would have argued more vehemently, except he was right that he could get up and down more easily from the futon than the sagging mattress in the bedroom that fought every attempt to escape it. She'd had to stick her head outside and ask the first person she saw—someone named Jack, she thought—to bring bedding and towels from the lodge. Actually, she said meekly, "Spencer wants some bedding for the futon, and, um, our towels are all bloody. I'm afraid to leave him yet. Do you think…?"

The guy complied.

Spencer refused to let her fetch help for him to go to the bathroom. Pain aged his face a decade or more as he pushed himself to his feet, leaning heavily on her. Two hours ago she'd never have considered that he could shuffle even this short distance on his own.

Needless to say, despite the fact that he was swaying in front of the toilet, he evicted her until he was done and flushed.

Around midday she did leave him alone long enough to walk to the lodge for food. She slipped in the back door, where all the women surrounded her and, whispering, demanded to know what had happened. Leah gave them the CliffsNotes version, then filled a bag with a few dishes, a saucepan and some silverware as well as sandwich makings, cans of soup and desserts. She didn't see a single one of the men as she hurried back to the cabin.

During her absence Spencer had gotten to a sitting position again on the edge of the futon. Stress on his face eased the minute he saw her.

"What took you so long?" he asked. With his lips grotesquely swollen, words were hard to make out, but Leah found she got the gist.

"I wasn't gone very long." She set down the two bags on the short stretch of counter next to the tiny sink. "Jennifer and everyone wanted to know about the fight. They were all ordered to stay in the kitchen and missed the whole thing."

"You get an update on Joe?" A note in his voice she didn't recognize had her turning to look at him.

"No. They served breakfast like usual, and when Lisa asked if she should take a plate up to Joe, Higgs snapped at her. Said he isn't in any shape to eat."

"He wouldn't be," Spencer agreed slowly.

Was he wondering if he *had* killed Joe? Or disturbed by the possibility of his death, however it came about? Yes, she decided, that was it. She wondered if, instead of becoming numb and inured to tragedy after all the death he'd seen, Spencer still had the capacity to grieve. There'd been nothing about Joe Osenbrock she could sympathize with, and yet... Who knew what his childhood had been like? What had made him so violently inclined and insecure enough to need so desperately to win?

And if Spencer's suspicion turned out to be true, she really hated the idea that one of those men she'd gotten to know was willing to steal upstairs in the lodge—perhaps to the very room where she'd been held captive—to break Joe's neck or slit his throat or... Leah didn't even want to think.

It bothered her even more to picture one of the men who'd protected her or helped Spencer today as the one willing to commit cold-blooded murder. Del? Shawn or Garrett? Chilled, Leah thought, *surely not Dirk Ritchie*. And yet...all of them intended to commit mass murder in the near future. Why balk at killing a single man?

"Will you eat something? I thought you might be able to drink soup from a cup."

"Not hungry."

She turned in alarm. What if the knife had reached his intestines or...maybe his liver or kidney? The pain relievers could have masked the effect that was only now catching up with him.

She evaluated him, deciding that his color was much better than it had been when they first carried him to the cabin. His eyes—well, eye—looked clear. If she made him open his mouth so she could look at his gums the way she would an injured dog's, would they be a healthy color or worrisomely pale?

"Will you try?"

He grunted and very carefully rested against the extra pillows Jack had included in the pile he brought from the lodge earlier. Spencer lifted each leg individually, using his good hand to guide it into place so he could stretch out. Only then did he say, "Yah."

She warmed cream of tomato, thinking it would go down easily and that milk would be good for him. When she took him a mugful and sat beside him to help prop him up, he did slowly drink it all.

Relieved, she had a bowlful herself.

She checked his watch, sitting on the old coffee table that had been pushed aside. "It's almost time for another painkiller. You won't try to be a tough guy and do without, will you?"

On a face that had suffered that much damage, it was hard to be sure, but she *thought* his expression was sardonic.

"No. Not tough."

When she gave him the pill half an hour later, he swallowed it, and after a period of staring broodingly up at the wood-paneled ceiling, dozed off. Leah tried to read but couldn't concentrate. Fictional adventures—or the very real ones during World War II—couldn't keep her attention when her current situation was so perilous.

Spencer was fighting his infirmities with a willpower that awed her. If the damage had been limited to the punches and bruising, however massive, she thought he'd be up and around in only another day or two. As it was, he'd lost a lot of blood, and she couldn't help fearing what harm that knife blade thrust between ribs might have done.

Had Spencer been ready for them to attempt an escape? He'd obviously learned a lot of what he'd been sent to find out. Now…how could they get away?

Was it possible for someone to get to any of the car keys?

Helen was the only one of the women Leah could imagine being willing to try to help her, but she wouldn't betray Dirk by helping Leah steal his truck, even if that was possible.

She and Spencer couldn't possibly set out on foot. Certainly not for days.

Her worries went round and round, but even when he was awake, she didn't vocalize them. Didn't need to. He was surely running the same scenarios and coming up with the same dead ends.

We should be okay for a few days, she told herself, but didn't quite believe her own assurance.

SPENCER HAD A hell of a time sleeping. No position was comfortable. Once Leah dropped off, she couldn't prevent herself from rolling into his aching body, or her arm would flop across his torso, and it was all he could do to stifle a bellow. Her head on his shoulder awakened sharp pain.

He didn't think he'd ever been battered from head to…not toe, calves before.

Come morning Spencer woke feeling as if he'd

just regained consciousness after being run over by a semi-truck with lots of huge tires. He tried not to move a muscle. Even breathing hurt. When he assessed his body, he found several places that felt like burning coals against the more generalized pain. Wrist, left cheekbone, the site of the stab wound, a searing strip down his thigh and his rib cage on the left.

All those could be managed, he convinced himself, and he knew from other times he'd taken a beating that the day after was the worst. Then the body would start healing itself.

Okay. One more day before he seriously considered an escape plan.

Leah stirred beside him and he had to grit his teeth. "Are you awake?" she whispered.

"Yah." His mouth was still swollen, making it difficult to shape words. But he got out the two that were most important. "Pain pills."

"What?"

He had to repeat himself before she said, "Oh, no! I should have woken you up earlier to take those. I'll get them right now."

She had to separate herself from him, the mattress rocking as she clambered out of bed. Teeth clenched, he held back the groans.

She hurried back. Sitting up enough to swallow the pills was agonizing. He needed the bathroom, but his bladder had to wait.

He caught glimpses as she got dressed, but as much as he normally enjoyed being tantalized by the fleeting sight of her curves, he didn't dare lift or even roll his head.

Wait.

It was a full half hour before the rigidity in his body eased enough, he was able to get up, shuffle to the bathroom and then lie down on the futon. As uncomfortable as the thing was, he needed to be out here where he could keep an eye on Leah and any possible entrances. He was able to half sit against the pile of pillows, so if something happened he could easily reach for his handgun.

Leah poached eggs for him and poured him a glass of orange juice. He was swallowing it when there was a polite knock on the door.

He called, "Who is it?" before Leah could reach the door.

"Del."

Spencer nodded at her and she let Del and Dirk in.

Del's gaze flicked to the gun then back to Spencer. "I'd say you look better, except…"

Spencer might have grimaced if that wouldn't have hurt. "Colorful?" he got out.

"Pretty as a rainbow," the other man confirmed. "You on your feet yet?"

"Sure." Spencer gave what was probably a death's head grin. "Hurt like hell today, though."

"Yeah, ain't that the way."

Dirk looked at Leah. "Anything you need?"

She succeeded in looking shy and even submissive. "I think we're okay. I went over to the lodge yesterday for some food and dishes. You know."

"Helen said you'd been by."

Spencer couldn't help asking. "Joe?"

Del answered, voice expressionless. "Died during the night."

Leah pressed her fingers to her lips to stifle a gasp. Both men glanced at her before returning their gazes to him. Dirk wasn't hiding his perturbation as well as Del was. He didn't like knowing Higgs had ordered—or even committed—the murder.

"Whatever I said about killing him, I didn't mean him to die," Spencer managed to get out.

Del obviously made out what he'd said because he nodded. "Figured. Ah…the colonel says he'll stop by later."

"Good. It'll be tomorrow before I can walk as far as the lodge." And, damn, he wished that wasn't true.

Leah saw the two men out, closed the door and waited through the thud of them descending the few steps before she turned around, distress on her face. "You were right."

"About Joe?" He was careful to sound…indifferent. "He wasn't in good shape when they hauled him away yesterday."

"Neither were you," she said tartly.

He let himself smile, although it couldn't look good. "I had the services of the only medic on site."

She opened her mouth, no doubt to remind him that she'd volunteered to look at Joe, too, but was again smart enough to let that remain unsaid.

"You were restless last night. Why don't you try to get some sleep?" she suggested.

He might do that. She'd wake him up soon enough when Higgs came calling. "You'll be here?"

"Won't go anywhere." She sketched a cross over her heart.

That made his misshapen mouth twitch.

He drifted in and out of sleep for much of the afternoon, helped along by the pain meds. Leah made sure he ate a little for lunch, and did wake him up midafternoon when Higgs came knocking.

He didn't have a lot to say, probably thanks to Leah's presence. "Shame about Joe," he remarked, his tone holding not a smidgen of regret.

Spencer met his eyes. "Sure is."

"We picked out a place to bury him. Can't let authorities get involved."

No shit. Couldn't let the body stay in the lodge long enough to start decomposing, either, Spencer reflected.

He stiffened when Higgs looked at Leah. "We're missing you in the kitchen. I suppose Spencer needs you today, but he should be on the mend by tomorrow. I'm hoping you'll make that cake again."

Her eyes glittered with dislike. Her acting had some limitations, it appeared. But she said, "I'll be glad to make it again."

Spencer spoke up. "I liked it, too."

To Higgs, she said, "Did Jennifer talk to you about picking huckleberries? We could make some great cobblers and pies with them, and stretch supplies, too."

He looked surprised. "No. I noticed some ripe berries. Wasn't sure whether they were edible."

"They're delicious. The mainstay for birds and bears and probably some other animals."

"I'll set it up," he said, glanced at Spencer and added, "Hope there's a big improvement by tomorrow."

Was that an order? Irritated, Spencer didn't show how he felt. "You and me both. I'm not built to sit on the sidelines."

A monster cloaked in an average body and mild manner, Colonel Higgs left. Spencer ground his teeth a few times to keep from verbally venting his anger.

Leah didn't like it, but he started doing some stretches and getting up to walk for a few minutes every half hour or so. They could not afford for him to stay down.

THE NEXT MORNING they took the short walk to the lodge slowly. Leah stayed close to him, but Spencer didn't reach for her. His face was so blank, she knew he was intent on hiding how much pain he was still in. Somehow, he walked evenly, betraying no need to favor one side or the other. He had allowed her to rewrap his wrist, and of course his face was at its worst: still swollen and vividly colored. The black eye was barely slitted, his mouth distorted.

Something like halfway, he said out of the blue, "Know how to hot-wire a car?"

"Hot-wire...?" She sounded startled. "Unfortunately, no. To tell you the truth, I'm completely ignorant where cars are concerned. Beyond how to start and drive them, of course."

He grunted.

"What are you thinking?"

"The Jeep." He'd mentioned it. "Want to get my hands on the key, but if I can't…" He frowned. "I can hot-wire it myself. Old vehicles like that are easy. Plus, the Jeep is back behind the lodge. We'd have a chance of getting a real head-start. I was thinking just in case."

Just in case he was dead or captive and she had to run by herself. Sick to her stomach, she said, "The Jeep is out if I'm on my own."

He nodded, almost matter-of-factly. "We'll make sure it doesn't come to that."

Oh, good. She was completely reassured. She didn't have a chance to comment, though, because Arne Larson emerged from his cabin and fell into step with them.

"Good fight," he said admiringly.

So much for what had appeared to be a friendship with Joe. This was a guy who wouldn't have felt at all squeamish watching one gladiator troop mop up the other in the Colosseum. Spencer put on a front of being unemotional about what he'd had to do in the army and now, with the FBI, but she didn't believe in it. He still had a human reaction to events and people. He must; she couldn't be falling for him if he didn't. He wouldn't be so ready to sacrifice himself for her.

As for Arne…she'd swear she saw a trace of envy and dislike in his eyes.

Spencer didn't comment, probably saving his energy for mounting the lodge steps.

He felt on edge all day, starting with finding out that Leah had been sent with two of the other women— Shelley and Lisa—to pick huckleberries.

"Galt will make sure no bears get 'em," Higgs told him, smirking.

"What's he going to do if a bear charges them?" Spencer asked.

"Shoot it, what else? What are you worrying about? Black bears are supposed to be afraid of people."

"Not all. And they're big enough to be dangerous, you know. Bullets from a handgun wouldn't even slow one down. And then there are the grizzlies. No matter what, you wouldn't want to get between any bear and her cub."

"Grizzlies? What are you talking about?"

Spencer looked at this idiot. "Grizzlies were re-introduced to the north Cascade Mountains years ago. They're around. I've seen plenty of pictures of them browsing through thickets of berries."

Not sure his slurred speech had gotten through, he was satisfied to see Higgs alarmed and studying the tree line covertly. Spencer instead looked around at the empty range. "I thought the others would be here."

"I had them stop to pick up the new rifles and ammunition."

He'd have to find a way to involve himself in returning the weaponry to the armory at lunchtime.

"You're pulling my leg, aren't you?" Higgs said suddenly.

"Pulling your leg?" Ah. "Nope. We'd have seen

any bears around if we'd been careless enough to leave out food."

Colonel Higgs scowled at him. "Why didn't you say something?"

Spencer pulled off surprised. He hoped, given the state of his face. "You'd already chosen this site. I assumed you'd done your research." He shrugged. "I've heard guys talking about bears. Anyone from the northwest would know."

"You're not from around here."

"No, but I've climbed mountains here and in Alaska." He let the silence draw out a little before adding, "You're right that bears are mostly shy. If you stumble on 'em, they can be a problem, but we make enough racket to warn them off."

But the women picking berries wouldn't be, unless they maintained a conversation, something that was unlikely with TJ Galt standing over them with his sneer and his Beretta M9A3 semiautomatic, a shade of brown that went with his favorite desert camo T-shirts and cargo pants. Spencer found his sartorial taste especially ironic since TJ was one of the few men here who had never served in the military.

"You up to trying out the new rifle?" Higgs asked. "I'd like your take on it."

"Tomorrow," Spencer said. "I'm one solid bruise right now. Getting up and down is a chore, and any recoil wouldn't help me heal."

Higgs accepted his answer, which made Spencer grateful that some of his injuries were so visible.

He did take one of the rifles that were supposedly

being tried out by army rangers. The balance was okay. The optics were as good as anything he'd used before, but not an improvement. He only said, "Interesting," staying noncommittal as he handed it back to Ken Vogel. Then he glanced around.

"Where's Fuller?" He frowned, realizing a couple of other men were missing, too.

"More supplies. Fuller took his wife along with Jones."

Damn it. What did they need so soon after the last shopping expedition? Only food? This group did eat like hungry locusts. Still… Spencer tried to remember what day he, Lisa and Del had gone down to Bellingham. They'd seriously stocked up. Wednesday, he decided after counting back. Only five days ago.

Mine is not to reason why, he thought flippantly, before remembering the rest of the quote. *Mine is but to do and die.*

That seemed to sum up his current situation all too neatly.

Chapter Thirteen

After giving the other women instructions on how to tell which berries were ripe, Leah kept a sharp eye out for bears while they picked. For what good advanced warning would do. Either a black or grizzly bear could outrun any human over a short distance, should it feel inclined.

She ignored TJ, even when he wandered by her.

Otherwise, as she plucked berries and dropped them into a plastic bowl, she pondered the others, starting with him and Shelley.

If he wasn't such an unpleasant man, TJ would have been attractive: tall, broad-shouldered, fit. He walked like an athlete, had medium brown hair and hazel eyes. His nose had clearly been broken at some point, which didn't detract from a handsome face... except she couldn't help thinking he'd probably deserved to be slugged. She was ashamed to find she actually hoped that was what had happened, rather than a collision on a soccer field or a baseball pitch delivered too high.

She had only enough abstract knowledge about

the dynamics in abusive relationships to understand why Shelley stayed with him. Real understanding eluded her. The dullness in that poor woman's eyes, her body language, the way she cringed whenever TJ came close... Leah would be willing to bet Shelley had grown up abused as a child, too, or at least watching her mother being hit by her father, or even by a succession of men. If somehow she escaped TJ, the odds were good she'd find another abusive man.

Jennifer was deferential around Tim, but not scared in the same way. Helen lit up when she saw Dirk. Lisa Dempsey... Leah was less sure about her. She wouldn't think of challenging Del or any man, but Leah had heard Lisa talking comfortably to him a few times, and his low voice as he actually talked to her, too.

It felt weird to imagine them all under arrest, diminished by convict uniforms and handcuffs, the women seeing their men only through glass if they stuck by them at all.

Shelley would, Leah knew, and Helen, too. The others...she was less sure.

How on earth had all these men gotten sucked into an objective so horrifying? She wanted to be able to hate them all, but discovered it wasn't that simple. Colonel Ed Higgs, she could hate. *He'd* dreamed up this evil, a betrayal of the nation that he had supposedly served. *He'd* recruited all these guys, who were fearful of a changing America but not necessarily fanatical until then. *He* could coolly and with a secret smile say, *Shame about Joe*, when he had ordered him to be executed.

Rick Metz…lacked personality. Did he need to be told what to believe? Maybe he'd been at loose ends until Colonel Higgs gave him a clear objective and whatever nonsense justifications he used.

She sifted through the names of the men she knew best, finding it harder than it should be to label them evil, or even bad. Del Schmidt pretty much ignored her, and Lisa sometimes shrank from him. Beyond that, he mostly seemed decent. He'd been courageous defending her. Same for Garrett Zeigler and Shawn Wycoff.

Except…she wondered if any of the three had been thinking about *her*. Maybe all they'd been doing was currying favor with Spencer while Shawn at least could enjoy poking a stick at Joe.

Dirk Ritchie seemed downright nice.

Arne Larson wasn't nice; Leah remembered him slamming her against the wall and groping her while leering. And she hadn't forgotten how brutally TJ Galt had tackled her when she tried to escape, slugging her before hauling her back to face Higgs, their unlikely alpha wolf, without a semblance of gentleness.

Gee, could that be why she hoped someone had, once upon a time, slugged *him* hard enough to permanently dent his nose?

There were others she definitely didn't like, and a whole bunch who treated the women as if they were barely useful. Did they really feel that way? Or were they just blending in, the way school children were sometimes cruel because they didn't have the courage to stand up and say no?

Spencer must know them all a whole lot better than

she did. Did he regret what would happen to some of these men? Or had he become inured from previous undercover investigations? Nobody was all bad or all good; she did believe that. Even though Spencer must use people he was investigating to achieve his objectives, he'd have to stay focused on the crime they'd been willing to commit—or *were* willing to commit, in this case.

"Leah!" A heavy hand gripped her shoulder and spun her around.

Wide-eyed, righting her bowl before the berries spilled, she realized it was TJ.

"What were you doing, spacing out?"

She knew what she had to do. Bow her head, hope her hair fell forward to partly veil her expression and grovel. "I'm sorry," she mumbled. "I...I was worrying about bears."

The other women stole surreptitious glances at their surroundings.

"Their bowls are full. Yours is, too," he said impatiently. "Time to get back. This is a waste of my time."

Except she knew perfectly well that all he'd do once they got back was lean against the wall in the kitchen and watch them with both contempt and suspicion.

She bobbed her head and hurried toward the lodge, Lisa and Shelley keeping pace with her, TJ silently following. So much for using a berry-picking expedition to make a run for it. That scheme had been downright delusional.

FROM PARTWAY DOWN the table during dinner, a low voice carried to Spencer.

"…get down where I can have internet access…"

He didn't turn his head, making himself depend on peripheral vision. For once Higgs hadn't taken a seat near him. Instead, he'd grabbed a place beside Tim Fuller, and they'd had their heads together ever since. Damn. Had Fuller and the others gone to Bellingham at all?

"Don't like losing you for two days…" Higgs's voice got drowned out. Surfaced again. "…think it's important enough."

Fuller's fervor made the hair rise on the back of Spencer's neck. Probably whatever nugget of information he so eagerly sought had nothing to do with Spencer or Leah—but there was a lesser chance that it did.

Higgs seemed unconcerned, though. Even talking quietly, his enthusiasm could be heard. "…more like the SAKO TRG 42…big jump forward from the…"

Spencer couldn't hear the rest, but didn't need to. The SAKO TRG 42 was a Finnish rifle, much admired among the sniper community. He knew guys who'd sworn by it. Except for the unusual stock design, which did indeed remind him of the SAKO, he couldn't say anything special had jumped out at him about this latest weapon sent to army spec ops for experimentation. Arms makers did that often. Most of those rifles didn't prove themselves any better than what snipers were currently using or regular infantry carried.

When Higgs called down the table, "You handled that baby, Spencer. Tell Fuller what you thought."

Spencer dredged up a few admiring comments that got all the men excited, even though most of them lacked the skills to take advantage of a cutting-edge weapon.

What worried him more was the disappearance this afternoon of two of the men along with Higgs. Spencer had seen them coming out of the makeshift armory, expressions satisfied. He knew from background checks that Ken Vogel had spent a decade on a police bomb squad, while Steve Baldwin had been expelled from Stanford's physics program for reasons no one had wanted to talk about. Another Ph.D candidate had hinted that he'd been caught walking out with materials too dangerous to let out of the secure labs.

Spencer knew how most of these men had hooked up with Higgs: the internet. As fast as one fringe site that urged violence and revolution was shut down, another popped up. Like recognized like. He'd also done enough research to know that quite a few members of the group had been at a crossroads in their lives when they saw an opportunity that gave them a sense of purpose.

Baldwin was one example. No other grad program would take him. He must already have been working out what he could do with his knowledge, education and possibly some stashed-away dangerous material. Vogel had just gone through a divorce during which his wife claimed he abused her and the children. His visitation with those kids was to be supervised. He'd have seen that as an unforgivable insult; not only an attempt to humiliate him but also to steal *his* children.

Higgs, of course, had been forced out of the military for his views. Likewise, Arne Larson, given a dishonorable discharge that would limit his job opportunities.

And so it went. TJ Galt had had an unapologetic, vile presence on alt-right websites for several years.

Spencer had to make guesses about a few of them. Leaving the military to find themselves qualified only for poorly paid, low-end jobs, maybe. Don Durand's wife had left him, too. Dirk Ritchie's father had disowned his "embarrassment" of a son.

Yeah, most of these guys had been desperate to latch on to something that would salvage their self-esteem, make them feel important. Not hard to understand.

They wouldn't like prison, he thought grimly.

Even if he was knocked out of the equation, the investigation had been going on long enough, and these men, the pawns, would go down. It would be a shame to see them taking the fall for the scum financing Higgs's great dream, or stealing munitions from the United States.

Dinner was ending, people drifting away as the women cleared the table. Spencer took his time finishing a sizeable piece of Leah's cake and his third cup of coffee. When Higgs, bringing his own coffee cup, slid down the bench to join him, Spencer said, "Did you see Durand today at the target range? He's showing a real knack." Which was, unfortunately, true. "I may try him out at two hundred yards tomorrow. Get him working on positional shooting. It's never safe to assume you can settle in prone and not have to move. Plus bullet trajectory, zeroing in and understanding his range finder." He paused. "Is there any reason to focus on night observation devices?"

"Shouldn't think so." Higgs mulled that over. "If we have time, it probably wouldn't hurt."

Apparently, the plans were still in flux. Or else Higgs knew his small army might find themselves pinned down into the night.

Spencer nodded.

Looking frustrated, Higgs asked, "Is Durand the only one with sniper potential?"

Spencer waggled a hand. "Jason Shedd is getting there. He wasn't a hunter and didn't have comparable experience to the others with a rifle coming in, but he does have patience, an understanding of things like bullet trajectory, and a soft touch. He just had further to go."

"Given his experience as a mechanic, some of that makes sense."

"You don't mind me cutting the two of them out of the herd for more intensive training?"

"No, I'm lucky to have you. Originally, I thought I had two other former snipers on board, but one of them…" He shook his head. "Art Scholler. He was too glib. I got a bad feeling."

"You think he wanted in undercover?"

"Yeah."

Art Scholler *was* FBI, although of course that wasn't his real name. Spencer had been brought in when Art got cut off cold.

"The other guy?"

"Didn't think he'd take orders. The guy had serious issues."

Spencer grunted. "After enough deployments, a lot of men bring home a cargo plane full of issues."

The colonel grimaced. "True enough. The anger is useful. The rest of it gets in the way."

From a man who'd been a member of the "Chair Force," Higgs's know-it-all attitude rubbed Spencer the wrong way. He knew plenty of airmen who'd been in war zones, but Higgs didn't impress him as one who'd gotten his hands, let alone his boots, dirty. As usual, he stayed agreeable and emphasized how invested he was as they discussed problems concerning a couple of other men on the team, including TJ Galt.

"He makes me think of a pit bull trained for fighting. Keeping him on a leash takes some effort," Higgs observed.

The guy did have a gift for reading people, which wasn't uncommon in predators. Talk about useful skills. In this case… Galt made no effort to hide his anger. If he had PTSD, it likely dated to his childhood. Spencer hadn't uncovered any adult trauma that would explain it.

They parted amicably, which didn't entirely settle the uneasiness Spencer felt, awakened by the half heard conversation. All he could do was pack it away with all his other worries. The weight of them, he thought, was like the kind of hundred-pound pack he'd once thought nothing of hefting. The cargo plane…well, he had other issues, too.

THE NEXT DAY passed in what Leah thought of as deceptive peace. Tim Fuller took off on some errand of his own, which surprised her. This was the first time since she'd been here that any of the men had left alone. Had he been sent to make phone calls for Higgs? Or might he have something personal he had to take care of? She had the uncharitable thought that he could have a meeting with his parole officer.

Along with the other women, she baked, cooked, cleaned and waited on the men. Her real life had come to be out of focus enough to seem hazy. She told herself she was better off that way. She was surprised when she counted back to realize she'd been here nine days. It seemed longer. Well, she couldn't afford to dwell on resentment or have an outbreak of rebellion.

Spencer couldn't afford for her to blow it, either. She suspected he was hurting a lot more than he let on, especially once he joined the other men. His eyes met hers briefly before a large group left for the shooting range. She read reassurance in that instant, but who knew?

In a few minutes the quiet would be shattered by the nonstop barrage. Were these guys really getting a lot more accurate, or were they just wasting ammunition and scaring wildlife for a mile or so around? It spoke to the isolation of the resort that nobody at all had heard the gunfire and reported it to the county sheriff's department or a ranger.

At lunchtime the men inhaled cheeseburgers, baked beans and apple pie *à la mode*. During the afternoon they seemed to break up into smaller groups for—who knew?—hand-to-hand combat training, lessons on stealth?

Or were some of them building a bomb?

That made her shiver.

Dinner was Jennifer's lasagna, loaves and loaves of garlic bread, and a grated carrot and raisin salad Leah made. It was sweet and substantial enough to appeal to men who wouldn't touch a green salad or plain broccoli, but still mostly qualified as a vegetable.

As if she cared about their nutritional intake. But everything she could do to blend in, to make herself valued, was good.

She was first setting out serving bowls when Tim Fuller walked in. Higgs didn't notice at first; Tim ended up sitting at the far end close to the women. The colonel glanced that way but didn't comment.

In her intense dislike, Leah thought, too bad the mythical parole officer hadn't found cause to lock up Tim and throw away the key. She must have smiled, because she discovered he was looking at her with an ugly expression. He and TJ Galt were two of a kind. With Joe Osenbrock, they'd made a vicious triumvirate.

With dinner over, Spencer stayed at the table with his usual refill of coffee, tonight talking to two men she hadn't had much to do with. Jason something and... She couldn't remember the other man's name at all.

The swelling in Spencer's face was going down, she noted, but the bruises had turned a multitude of colors. As she poured coffee from the carafe into Jason's cup, Spencer was saying something about wind, his speech much clearer than it had been even that morning.

The three of them weren't alone; a bunch of the men lingered, happy to hang out with friends, she gathered. During her last trip around the table to refill coffee cups, she shivered at the way several of the men watched her. She wasn't *afraid* of them, exactly—certainly not with Spencer present—but she could tell what they were thinking, and it gave her the creeps.

If there was another demand for more coffee, one of the other women could handle it. Clearly, Spencer wouldn't be ready to go for a while yet, so once she put leftovers away in the commercial refrigerator, she borrowed a sweatshirt hanging on a hook and slipped outside. She'd stay close to the door so she could hear Spencer calling for her. She knew eventually someone would notice she was out here. Sometimes, the other women took breaks like this, only to be chased inside when one of the men came to check on them.

The crisp evening air felt good, and when she tipped her head back, she saw the first stars appearing against a deep purple sky.

It had to be a lot later than usual, to be already getting dark. Fine by her; her new domestic tasks didn't exhaust her, but she'd barely sat down today except for perching on the bench to gobble each meal. Besides…she'd seen a glint in Spencer's eyes when his gaze strayed her way while she was wiping down the table. If he was feeling better enough…

Uncle Edward had built a couple of crude benches back here, wide boards laid over cut-off tree stumps.

She chose one and sat, knowing she was almost hidden in the shadow of a cedar that would soon have to be cut down if the lodge was to survive. The roots probably already burrowed beneath the foundation.

Male voices drifted to her, abruptly becoming louder. Leah stiffened, ready to hustle back in the kitchen door if they came any closer.

One of them was Ed Higgs's, she realized.

"You're *sure*?" It was a demand; he didn't want to believe whatever he'd been told.

"Positive. It took some serious searching, but I found a picture. He was coming out of a courthouse, wearing the typical FBI getup."

She quit breathing. *Oh no, oh no.*

Tim Fuller was ebullient, really glad to be able to bring down a man he'd deeply resented. "You know," he continued, "black suit, white shirt, shiny black wingtips, blue tie. He was identified as Special Agent Alex Barr. Chicago office then. Now, I don't know."

"God damn." Anger threaded Higgs's weariness. "I can't believe it."

"Believe it," Tim said. "I printed the picture. Left it in my cabin."

Leah rose to her feet and began feeling her way toward the two steps up to the kitchen door. She stopped just short. No—the minute she opened it, light would spill out. Slip all the way around the lodge, she decided. Spencer might have only minutes.

The last few words she heard before going around the corner of the old log building were "no choice."

Chapter Fourteen

Spencer had stood to go looking for Leah when the front door opened. He turned automatically to see who'd come in. It was her, and the flat-out terror he saw on her face had even the hair on his arms rising. An instant later she'd mostly blanked that out, and he hoped the two men with him hadn't seen her naked emotion.

"I'm ready to head back to the cabin," he said easily. "See you two in the morning. We'll do some more work on setting up shots from different vantage points."

Both appeared eager. Neither had let ego get in the way of learning all they could from him. Amidst the "good-nights," he walked toward Leah.

"Ready to go?"

"Yes." The tremor in her voice would have had him on full alert even if he hadn't already shot straight to maximum readiness. He took her arm as they went out the door and descended the stairs. Then, seeing no one, he bent his head and asked softly, "What's wrong?"

"They know." It tumbled out of her. "Even your real name. Tim told Higgs he'd found a photo of you coming out of a courthouse somewhere."

"Where were they?"

"Out back."

The wheels in his head spun. "We don't dare go back to the cabin." He started hustling her in the opposite direction, to the nearest tree line. Thinking aloud, he said, "The Jeep."

"But…it's dark. And don't you need some tools to hot-wire it?"

"Got the key today," he said, more grateful than he could remember being for anything, except maybe seeing an unconscious Joe Osenbrock being carried away. He still didn't like their only option. The minute anyone heard the sound of the engine being fired up in back, the hunt would be on.

Their best hope, he concluded, was that neither Higgs nor Fuller had had a chance to spread the word. The other guys would wonder, maybe think someone was using the Jeep to drive out to the range to collect something that had been forgotten earlier.

The longer the hesitation, the more chance he and Leah would have to make a clean getaway.

The bigger, more powerful vehicles wouldn't have much, if any, advantage over the Jeep during the first mile or two. The rutted, winding gravel road on the edge of that steep plunge to the river had to be taken with care no matter how hot the driver was to catch someone ahead of him. Unfortunately, he'd have to drive cautiously, too.

Once past that stretch, they'd be overtaken quickly unless they got a big enough head start.

A plan forming in his head, he said, "We have to go for the Jeep. Pray nobody noticed the missing key."

Leah didn't say anything, just jogged at his side. He was glad to see that she'd put on a sweatshirt over her T-shirt; borrowed, he thought. He didn't have any equivalent, which meant he'd be damn cold at night, but the temperature hadn't dropped below freezing anytime this past week, so they should be all right.

He didn't want to even think about how long it would take for them to walk out to the closest neighbor or tiny town where someone might have a working telephone. Shit, why hadn't he kept his own with him, even if it was useless up here? He might have had coverage before they got as far as Glacier or Maple Falls.

Or…what would happen if they headed north for the border? He tried to envision a map, but had a bad feeling that was even rougher country. And it wasn't as if they'd know when they reached the border, or that the entire thing was patrolled 24/7. No towns or highways within remotely easy reach of where they'd emerge, either.

At least heading for the Mount Baker highway, they'd be going downhill. Given his condition, that was a real positive if they had to eventually go on foot.

He stopped Leah as close to the armory as they could get without stepping out in the open. As they stood in silence, he searched the ground between them and the lodge. The only movement was the dart of bats. A faint "whoo" came to his ears from somewhere behind them.

"Okay," he murmured, "I want you to turn around and go back to the head of the road leading out of here." The moon had risen enough to let her see where he was pointing. "When I get there, I'll stop for you to jump in."

"Why don't I just get in the Jeep with you now?" she asked.

He shook his head and talked fast. "There's a chance they'll be waiting for me. If so, you need to take off on your own. You can't follow the road— they'll find you. Traveling in the dark is hard, but try to get a ways before you hide. Got that? I know you can do it. You know this area, wildlife. Better than they do."

"Do you really think we can outrun them?" she whispered.

"No, but I have a plan for that, too."

She pressed her lips together, but nodded instead of arguing as he felt sure she wanted to. Her resistance to the idea of abandoning him to save herself was a part of why he'd fallen for her so fast.

Right now all he did was give her a quick, hard kiss and a push. "Go."

She went, slipping away and disappearing more quickly in the thick darkness beneath the big trees than he'd expected.

He had no choice but to cross the thirty yards or so of open ground to reach the back of the armory. Hating to be so exposed, he did it at a trot. Reaching the back wall, he flattened himself against it, pulled his Sig Sauer and took a moment to slow his breathing.

Then he slid like a shadow around the side, instinct throwing him back to when he'd been a soldier, letting him place his feet soundlessly.

There were no voices. The only light came from lodge windows and, more diffused, the first cabins. The Jeep sat where it had been since Higgs moved it out of the building.

Spencer stepped from the cover of the building, just as another man appeared from where he'd hidden behind the low branches of one of the old cedars. Spencer froze, weapon trained on the man.

"Is what Fuller says true?" asked Dirk Ritchie.

Finger tightening on the trigger, Spencer sweated over what to do. If he fired, men would pour out of the lodge. And, damn, he didn't want to kill Dirk.

"How did you know I'd be out here?"

"I saw you take the key," Dirk said simply. His hands remained at his sides, even though he was carrying, too.

"Did you?" Spencer said tensely. "You and Helen need to take off, too. Use the confusion after I'm gone."

Dirk stayed quiet.

Spencer pitched his voice low, yet filled it with intensity. "Do you really want to be party to slaughtering what might be hundreds of people who are just thinking about going to their kids' parent-teacher meetings, or the guy they just met, or a sick parent?

Remember the Oklahoma City bombing that killed *fifteen* preschooler children?"

Somebody else would come out any minute. He had to *go*.

He took the last steps to the Jeep. "Stop me, or don't."

Only a few strides separated the two men now. Shooting Dirk would feel like murder, but if he didn't—

Dirk stepped back. "Get out of here."

"Thank you."

The other man turned and walked toward the lodge, not hurrying. Switching his attention to the Jeep, Spencer had a sickening thought. What if Dirk had told Higgs he'd seen Spencer pocket the key? What if the Jeep had already been disabled?

He couldn't hesitate. Didn't have time to think of a Plan B. What were the chances he'd make it to the tree line? Gripping the overhead bar above the seats, Spencer swung himself in behind the wheel, grimacing as the quick movement tugged at his stitches and ignited pain in his ribs. No need to open or close a door. He pulled the key from his pocket, inserted it, held his breath and turned it.

The engine roared to life.

The porchlight above the back door into the kitchen came on. A voice called out.

He put the Jeep in gear and slammed his foot down on the gas pedal.

LEAH HADN'T QUITE reached the meeting place when she heard the engine start. Spencer had gotten that far. Thank God. Thank God.

Running, she crossed the weedy gravel to reach the other side and turned to see the Jeep racing toward her. The headlights switched on just before he came even with her. He braked, she grabbed for the door handle and yanked. Metal squealed, but the door refused to give way.

"Jump in."

What she did was fall in, but it worked. The Jeep was rocketing forward long before she untangled herself enough to sit up. If there was a seat belt, her groping fingers didn't find it. Instead, she gripped the edge of the seat with one hand and flattened the other on the dashboard.

The feeble, yellow beams cast by the headlights didn't illuminate the road ahead more than ten or fifteen feet.

"I hope you know this road," she heard herself gasp.

"I do."

He'd been aware from the beginning that there was the possibility he'd have to run for it, she supposed, which meant being ultra-observant about little details like the only outlet from the resort. Spencer sounded awfully tense, though.

"Do you hear—?"

He didn't have to finish. Yes, deep-throated engines had been started. Aside from her own car, every vehicle she'd seen up here dwarfed this old Jeep. The giant SUVs and pickups could almost run right over the top of it.

She craned her neck to see behind her. Bright lights appeared.

Spencer mumbled a few obscenities.

"You have a plan." How did she sound even semi-calm? The cold wind whipped her hair and made her eyes water. Gravel crunched beneath the tires. She dreaded the moment when they reached the stretch above the river.

She ought to be thankful it was dark, and she wouldn't be able to see the valley floor.

"I'm going to take a few curves," he said tersely, "brake long enough for you to leap out and run for the woods, then try to set up a skid so that the Jeep goes over the edge and down into the river. They'll think we screwed up."

"What if you can't jump out?" she said numbly.

"I don't have time to try to find a heavy enough rock to brace the accelerator."

"There's something behind the seat." She'd caught a glimpse when she was facedown after her tumble into the Jeep. She didn't know what she'd seen, but now she got on her knees and felt down in the cavity. "I think it's a car battery. They're heavy, aren't they?"

"Yes. Damn. That should work. Can you pick it up?"

"I think so." Her position was completely un-safe, crouched instead of sitting while trying to heft a heavy object between the seat backs. If he started that skid too soon… Laughter almost bubbled up. Unsafe. *Right*.

She tugged and rocked it until she got her fingers

beneath the rusty metal, and then twisted, plunked onto her butt and lowered the battery to her lap.

She sensed Spencer's quick glance.

"We're coming up on a good place to let you out. Just beyond, there's a gap where the guardrail has rusted and broken. That's what I'll aim for."

Leah's head bobbed as if she was just fine with any of this. "You'll find me?"

"Yes." He braked, skidded enough to have him swearing again and stopped. She scrambled over the door, leaving the battery on the seat. He accelerated again before she started running.

THIS WOULD ALL be for nothing if the Jeep hung up on a stubbornly intact stretch of guardrail, but he had no time to waste to scout ahead to be sure he knew where the break was. All Spencer could do was judge distances from his memory.

Here.

He braked, cranked the wheel hard, then lifted the battery over the gearshift. Got out.

The sound of approaching engines was too loud. No time.

He slipped the gearshift into Neutral and shoved the battery down on the accelerator at almost the same moment. The Jeep leaped forward, the open door whacked him and he tumbled free.

Without looking to see if he'd succeeded, he ran full out for the bank on the uphill side of the road and scrambled up it. There, he paused only momentarily, turning. The Jeep had disappeared, the sound of its engine drowned out by approaching vehicles. Had the steering somehow corrected itself?

Then he heard metal tearing, screaming in agony… followed by an unholy explosion.

Just as the first set of headlights illuminated that stretch of road he faded back into the forest.

DEEP IN THE TREES, Spencer couldn't see any better than he would have in a cavern a mile below the ground. He should have set up some kind of plan for him and Leah to find each other when separated. If she didn't stick pretty close to the road, it would take sheer luck for them to stumble onto each other.

Swearing silently as the receding shouts faded behind him, he made his way uphill, trying to stay twenty feet or so from the road. If the sound of pursuit reached him, he wouldn't be able to keep doing that. At least he could be assured he *would* hear anyone chasing him on foot; it was impossible to pass through the tangle of vegetation without making some noise.

Something swiped him in the face. He shook his head and spun. A swag of lichen, pale even in the limited light, still swayed.

He had a memory of telling Leah *not* to follow the road if she had to take off on her own. Surely to God she'd use common sense and realize they didn't have a prayer of finding each other if she didn't.

He kept moving, pausing every ten feet or so to listen.

Uphill, he heard a muffled cry. Animal? Bird? Some thrashing followed.

Moving as quietly as he could, he headed that direction. What if she'd hurt herself? he thought suddenly but pushed the fear aside.

Quiet closed around him. Maintaining any orientation took determination, and Spencer wouldn't swear he wasn't veering off a straight line toward a sound that could have been a porcupine waddling through the forest, or a bear crashing on its way.

Guessing himself to be close, he finally said, "Leah?" All he could do was hope he wasn't too close to the road—and that Higgs hadn't been smart enough to have men walking it, listening and watching for any indication that someone was in there and not dead on the rocky bank of the low-running river.

"Spencer?"

"Hold still."

She didn't answer. He stepped forward carefully. He felt renewed irritation at himself; if he'd had his phone, he'd have also had a flashlight—although he wouldn't have dared use it now.

He put out a foot and found only space, teetering before he drew back.

A woeful whisper came from the darkness. "I fell in."

Spencer crouched. His eyes had adjusted well enough for him to see fern fronds waving wildly. Presumably, they disguised a hollow. Maybe a giant tree stump had rotted into nothingness; who knew?

"I'm here," he murmured. "Are you hurt?"

"I don't think so."

"Okay." Relief flooded him. He held out a hand. "Can you see me?"

"Yes." More stirring among what he thought was mostly lush clumps of sword ferns. A slim hand seized his, and he exerted steady pressure until she scrambled out of the hollow and fell against him.

Her arms wrapped his torso even as he held her tight, ignoring the pain in his wrist.

Against his chest, she mumbled, "I was so scared! And afraid I couldn't find you, and—"

Exhilarated because they *had* found each other, he chuckled. Her hair stirred against his cheek.

"I was getting a little worried myself," he admitted.

Her head came up. "What *happened*?"

"The Jeep sailed over the cliff and exploded when it hit the rocks at the bottom. Last I knew, the SUVs coming up behind us stopped there. I heard voices. Whether they bought it entirely… I don't know. I'm betting they don't find a way to get to the Jeep until daylight, though. Whether they're taking into account the possibility we weren't in the Jeep, I don't know."

After a moment she nodded. "Now what?" she asked, sounding as if she was running through options in her head.

That was an excellent question. From where they stood, downhill would take them southeast. They'd almost have to hit the highway. Even so, he'd give a lot for a topographical map. And, hey, food, warmer clothes, possibly a sleeping bag, the flashlight and phone, the absence of which he'd already regretted, and probably a lot of other things that hadn't yet occurred to him but would as soon as he or Leah needed them.

He winced. Like the bottle of pain meds. Except, he'd stuck two of them in his pocket, meaning to take them with dinner but decided not to show his vulnerability so publicly. He'd hold out as long as he could before taking them one at a time.

Preferably after they came on at least a trickle of water.

Right now...

"Two choices. Keep going, away from the road. Or hunker down for the night. If we're going to do that, you found us a great place to hide."

He kind of thought she made a face before saying, "I agree. What's your preference? You okay?" She glanced at his still-bandaged wrist.

Reluctantly, he said, "I'm fine. I think we move on. We're too close to the road here. By morning, if not sooner, they'll be looking for us. I haven't had the impression that any of them are real outdoorsmen. A few say they've hunted, so maybe I'm wrong. Still, most outdoor experience doesn't prepare you for a temperate rain forest."

"Have *you* ever spent any time in the north Cascades?"

"Yeah, did some climbing here years ago." Over the course of several leaves, a buddy, Aaron, and he had ascended seven mountains altogether, from the Rockies to the Teton Mountains and here in the Cascades. Spencer hadn't gone climbing since Aaron had been killed in a firefight.

"What about bears? I know what they can do, remember."

He decided not to remind her about porcupines, also nocturnal. "They're rarely aggressive with humans, as you know."

After a minute Leah straightened away from him. "I'm ready."

Conscious of his many aches and the sharp pain in his side and thigh and wrist, he'd have liked to sleep for a few hours. But he wouldn't feel any better tomorrow morning, the next day, or the next. Even a little distance covered tonight would give them a head start tomorrow.

He nodded and led the way, hoping like hell he was going approximately in the right direction—and that they wouldn't stumble out on the winding road where someone might be waiting for them.

The parable about the blind leading the blind crossed his mind. Aesop? Just as well he couldn't remember how that story ended.

Chapter Fifteen

Because of his recent wounds and undoubted pain, Leah insisted they take regular breaks to rest. He didn't argue, but gave away his tension by regularly pushing a button on his watch to check the time. She didn't bother asking how long they'd been on their way, and he didn't offer the information. The day's stresses had caught up with her ages ago—and if she found out that was really only half an hour ago, she might scream—but really she was grateful to be so tired; she couldn't do any concentrated worrying. She just followed in Spencer's wake, knowing at least that she wouldn't tumble into another hole unless he did first.

The ground was soft and uneven, though. Squishy in places, more from the depth of the moss and decomposing organic matter. They clambered over and walked around fallen trees, some that might have come down last winter, others already rotting and serving as nurse logs for saplings. In some of those places faint rays of moonlight found them, and she glimpsed tiny distant stars. Much of the time enormous trees reared above them, blocking out the sky. She had a vague memory of Uncle Edward talking about some true old-growth forest close by and wondered if that was what this was.

It might be, because at some point the walking became easier since they weren't having to fight the ferns and salmonberries and who-knew-what that scratched and tripped them. The darkness was almost absolute, the boles of standing trees enormous. Not that the ground didn't remain uneven, the extreme dark hiding obstacles that would cause Spencer to growl under his breath before he helped her around or over them.

She walked right into him when he stopped.

"I'm beat," he said. "I suggest we get on the other side of this log and try to sleep a little."

Since she was very close to sleepwalking, Leah thought she could do that. And she knew Spencer must be dead on his feet to actually admit to needing a rest.

They had to go around this time. Taking her hand, he guided her. The trunk must have been six or eight feet in diameter. Even decomposing, it reared above her head. On the back side, he advanced slowly before stopping, seeming to feel his way. "This looks as good as anyplace."

Looks? *She* couldn't see a thing, but she wasn't about to quibble, either.

Once she'd squatted and then plunked down, she tried very hard not to think about what insects inhabited a rotting log. Would there be snakes around?

Not poisonous ones, she was pretty sure. Her hand bumped something that sort of…crumbled. Recoiling, she made out a lighter shape against the dark backdrop of loam and moss. Mushrooms. Now, *those* could be poisonous, but she didn't plan to eat one.

She heard a groan as Spencer carefully lowered himself beside her. Oh, heavens—she should have helped him. Given the possibly broken wrist, he wouldn't lean any weight on that arm, and the gash in his thigh had to hinder him.

Too late.

"God, this feels good," he said after a minute.

"Uh-huh." Except she felt herself listing sideways until she came up against his big, solid body. "Can we lie down?" She was slurring.

"We can."

They shifted, she squirmed, he wrapped her in his arms and they ended up prone. He spooned her body from behind. His arm made a perfect pillow. Her eyelids sank closed, she mumbled something that was supposed to be "good night" and fell asleep.

CRADLING THIS WOMAN he suspected he loved, Spencer wasn't as quick to drop off to sleep.

When things went to shit, it happened fast.

If not for the damn fight, he'd be in a lot better physical shape and thus more confident that he and Leah would make it safely out of this densely wooded, uninhabited forest. If he'd had even ten or fifteen minutes' warning, he could have filled a pack with food, first-aid supplies, flashlight and more. As it was, they were screwed if either of them so much as developed blisters on their feet. His boots protected his ankles, while Leah's athletic shoes were fine for walking, but wouldn't keep her from turning an ankle.

They just about had to move during the daytime rather than at night even though they might be spotted. Especially given their physical condition, they had to be able to see where they were stepping. In fact, they were lucky no disaster had already occurred with them blundering around in the dark.

He cast his mind back to that brief encounter with Dirk. Spencer had had no idea he'd been seen pocketing the key. If it had been anybody but Dirk…if Dirk had told Higgs, or when he saw Spencer at the Jeep had opened his mouth and yelled… No point in going there now.

He hoped Dirk *had* kept his mouth shut and did find a way to take off.

His thoughts jumped again.

How the hell had that idiot Fuller stumbled on the photo?

He actively tried not to be photographed. With the press sticking their noses in everywhere, he'd been unable to completely evade them given that he had to testify in court. Most outlets were good about not publishing those pictures, but he knew of a couple that had made it into newspapers or TV news stories. There were undoubtedly more online. In fact, the one Tim Fuller had described in Leah's hearing had to be one of those.

His ascendancy in Higgs's estimation had rubbed Tim, in particular, wrong for months. But had he made mistakes that gave away his law-enforcement background? Spencer shook his head slightly. He had no idea, and at this point that was irrelevant. Permanently irrelevant, if he declined to go undercover again.

Tim had to have sensed/heard/seen something to make him do that kind of online prowling. Or, hell, had he contacted a friend who was more of a computer wizard? Maybe, Spencer concluded.

For all that things had gone to shit, he and Leah had made their getaway and, right now, were fine. They wouldn't starve to death in the next two or three days.

The tricky moment would be when they had to approach a road.

He nuzzled Leah's silky hair and let sleep claim him.

HIS BODY'S DEMAND awakened him before Leah had so much as moved. In fact, it didn't appear either of them had made any of the restless shifts in position normal to sleepers. Her head still rested on his biceps; he still spooned her.

He'd have enjoyed the moment if he didn't need to empty his bladder, and if his body wasn't reporting multiple other complaints. His shoulder ached, his arm was stiff, his wrist felt broken, his thigh throbbed and his whole left side was on fire. In a general way, he felt like crap. What if he was coming down with a cold or the flu?

Stuffing a groan back down where it came from, he gently shook Leah. "Time to rise and shine."

She whimpered, stirred and whimpered again. "I'm stiff. Although I don't know why I'm whining. You're the one who is injured."

He didn't say so, but he dreaded getting up.

Leah did get to her hands and knees, then to her feet. She suddenly said, "I need—" and bolted for a nearby tree.

Since he'd rather she not see him dealing with his infirmities, he got up, too, in slow increments. Water or no water, he was taking one of those damn pills. Just as she reappeared around the tree, he shuffled toward a different one.

There, he used the facilities, then did some stretches before returning to Leah.

"Turns out GrubHub can't find us to deliver that Denny's breakfast," he said. "Guess we'll have to do without."

Her smile rewarded him. "There are berries ripe, if we can find a clearing."

"Stumble on one, you mean."

"At least we can *see*."

That was an improvement, he'd concede.

He started out. He got the pill down, but was left with a foul taste in his mouth. Walking loosened muscles, and the pill did some good, too, but he felt as if someone was stabbing his thigh with a red-hot poker. All he could do was block out what he couldn't change and go on.

By the time sunlight made it to the forest floor, it was diffuse, soft, even tinted green-gold. He still had to watch carefully for the best places to set down his feet, which made for slow going. Common sense did battle with a sense of urgency; what if finding out they were being dogged by the FBI inspired Higgs to launch an early attack?

Helplessness didn't sit well with Spencer, but practically, there wasn't a damn thing he could do to prevent any immediate action Higgs took. He doubted a bomb had actually been built, but the debacle during the Boston Marathon had demonstrated how much damage could be done by really primitive bombs. He was afraid Ken Vogel, with his bomb squad experience, could put together any number of lethal explosive devices even without input from a budding physicist with an interest in nuclear fission.

Until he got his hands on a phone, he had no way to alert his office that the operation had blown up on him.

Then focus on the moment. Except for my aching body. Best not to think about that.

Deciding it was time for a short break, he spotted a moss-covered rock more or less the right height to let them sit.

Once they did so, Leah looked at him with worry in her eyes. "What do you think they're doing?"

"Right now?" He checked his watch. "Struggling

upriver to the wreck. That'll take them at least a couple of hours from the best place to leave vehicles."

"And then?"

Trust her to echo his concerns.

"I think there are two logical options for Higgs. One is to pack up and leave, probably have the others disperse until he can line up an alternate place for them to train. The other is to go for an immediate attack."

"Immediate?"

"Once he realizes we're on foot, he may decide to have the men hunt us for a day or two. Catching us would solve their problem with timing." He didn't have to say, *executing us.* "Otherwise, he could pull together a plan for an attack that might not be quite as spectacular as he intended, but those rocket launchers alone give him the firepower to threaten a gathering of politicians or even the president himself."

"You know him. Which is more likely?"

He didn't hesitate. "Dispersing. He likes the pieces to fit together. He'll want the big bang, so to speak. To accomplish that, the attack was to take place on a lot of levels. Bomb or bombs, rocket launchers, snipers picking off counterattackers or survivors trying to get away. Maybe even sending in a squad of men who don't have the range to be snipers to mow people down."

Leah looked more horrified by the minute. "That's why he wanted you."

"He needed a sniper to train others. That's what I was doing."

The urgency tapped on his shoulder, and he rose to his feet. "I'll stiffen up if we stop for long. Let's get going."

They continued in silence, Spencer straining to hear any sounds unnatural for the forest. Every now and again, a bird would flit by, most unidentifiable, a few common enough he recognized them, like the crow and later a jay, although that had unfamiliar coloration. They weren't plagued by a lot in the way of insects. Mosquitoes and even flies would prefer moist areas, butterflies open meadows with flowers. The rotting logs were no doubt rife with crawly things, centipedes, sow bugs and the like. Nothing that stung, as far as he knew.

And, on a glass half-full note, it wasn't raining. He knew from experience that rain wasn't uncommon here even in July and August. Some water to drink would be welcome; in fact, thirst was increasingly making itself known. But getting wet and having to keep going, pants chafing their legs, even socks soaked, that could be miserable.

"I hear something," she whispered.

He stopped and cocked his head. Speak of the devil. That had to be running water.

He turned, held a finger to his lips and progressed with even greater care. The small stream they found took enough of a tumble over rocks to have caused the delicate rippling sound. A deer that had been drinking saw them and bounded away.

"Oh, my."

"This water will likely make us sick," he told her,

dredging through his memory. "Giardia is the problem, as I recall. If we could boil it…"

She wrinkled her nose. "No stove handy."

"Nope. I don't think symptoms will catch up with us for at least a week or two." He hoped that recollection was accurate. "We'll need to ask for treatment once we have a chance to see a doctor."

If she doubted that time would come, she didn't comment.

Spencer splashed his face to cool it, and wished for a water bottle, too.

If wishes were horses…

His head had begun to throb. He debated taking the last pill now versus waiting, deciding on the latter. He might need it more come morning.

LEAH'S STOMACH GROWLED. She pressed a hand to it, hoping Spencer hadn't heard. He had enough to worry about, and given the toll his injuries took, he needed fuel for his body even more than she did.

He'd gotten quieter as the day went on, too. Pain tightened his face whenever he didn't remember to hide it. The flush she saw on his lean cheeks above dark stubble made her more uneasy. Even with all the willpower in the world, pushing himself to get back on his feet as soon as he did couldn't have been good for his recovery. She'd known all along that his risk of infection was high. She'd been able to don sterile latex gloves, and the gauze, scissors, needle and suturing material were sterile, too. Unfortunately, the blade of that black-handled knife Joe had used on him wasn't. Then there were the dirty shirts used to stem the bleeding. This was an awful time for the infection to appear. Dumb thing to think—was there a time that would have been *good*? If only there'd been antibiotics in that first-aid kit, or Spencer had stocked them along with the pain meds.

He was capable of going on with a fever, at least for now, Leah convinced herself. But what if they hadn't found their way out of the wilderness two days from now? Three?

He did go on, and on, hours upon hours, until her thighs burned and she'd quit thinking about anything but the next step. She'd thought of taking the lead but decided against it. With Spencer in front, he was more likely to stop when he needed it, while she might misjudge his stamina.

Just then Spencer stopped, Leah stumbling to a halt just before she walked into him. Blinking, she realized the light had changed without her noticing, deepening into purple.

"We risk getting injured if we continue in the dark," Spencer said, his voice rough. "I'm sorry we didn't come across any berries."

She took the hand he held out. "Going without for a day or two isn't that big a deal. Isn't fasting supposed to be good for you?"

"I've read that. I'm not convinced."

"Me, either." Studying him anxiously, she said, "I should look at your wounds while there's still some light."

"Why?" He let her go and lowered himself to another mossy piece of ground with a few pained grunts he apparently couldn't hold back.

"Why? Because—" She didn't finish.

"I'm not sure we even dare wash the wounds out in a stream," he said wearily. "What if that introduces different microorganisms into my body? And, in turn, I'd be introducing bacteria into the stream that might be deadly to fish or mammals downstream that drink out of it. What's more—" he continued inexorably "—we have no supplies to rewrap my wounds and especially my ribs."

The ribs might be hurting him more than anything, she realized. The binding did offer some support. Yes, she could tear her T-shirt into strips, say, but the knit fabric would be too stretchy to provide the same kind of support.

"I'm sorry." She sank down beside him. "I wish I could do something."

"I'll be okay. I just wish—" He shook his head as if regretting having said that much.

"Wish?" Leah prodded.

"I was sure I'm not leading us astray."

"Short of your watch converting into a compass, I don't see how you can know. You're not Superman, Spencer." Then she stopped again and frowned. "Why am I still calling you that?"

"You don't have to." With a sigh, he rolled his head. "But I might not answer to Alex."

"Really?"

He managed a smile. "No, I'm kidding, but I've

even been thinking of myself as Spencer. It's like... Do you speak a foreign language?"

"I'm pretty fluent in Spanish."

"You think in it when you're speaking it, right?"

"Yes."

"When I go undercover, I immerse myself to that extent. I'm not Special Agent Alex Barr. I *am* Spencer Wyatt. I can't slip."

"I can see that," she said slowly, even as she wondered how he could possibly do that. He'd said something once about not being sure who he was anymore, and how he'd done things, bad things, he didn't name. Not raped women, she felt certain. If he'd beaten men to death, or shot them, she believed he'd had adequate provocation.

Apparently losing interest in the subject, he said, "I think I'd like to lie down."

He let her help him, which said a lot about his condition. He encouraged her to join him, and soon they were curled up together. As the temperature dropped with nightfall, he had to be cold on top of everything else—unless he was burning up, of course. Leah rubbed his bare arms and lifted his hands to her skin beneath her sweatshirt. That he didn't protest told her how lousy he felt.

She kept thinking about a man who'd spent—she didn't know—much of the past several years, at least, undercover with violent fanatics who wanted to remake the country into their twisted ideals. She hadn't heard any slurs from him, as she had from some of the other men, but he must know all the right things to say to allow him to blend in.

How jarring it must be to return to his real life, whatever that was. An apartment? How homey was that, when it stayed empty for months on end? He presumably had no pets, he'd said he wasn't close to family and she didn't believe he had a girlfriend or fiancée waiting patiently for him. Spencer Wyatt—no, Alex Barr —wasn't the kind of man to make promises to one woman and have sex with another.

Feeling him relax into sleep, she thought, *I do know him. Of course I do.*

He'd been willing to give his life for her. That said enough about him to erase even fleeting doubts.

Hunger pushed off sleep for another while, but she was exhausted enough to drop off eventually.

Waking suddenly, the darkness unabated, she lay very still. What had disturbed her…? The answer came immediately. A wave of convulsive shivering seized Spencer. His back arched and his teeth chattered before he could clamp them shut.

Terrified, she realized there wasn't a single thing she could do except hold him, and keep holding him.

Chapter Sixteen

A murky haze that made Leah think of smog had settled over the usually crystal-clear silver-gray of Spencer's eyes. Or maybe it was more like a film. All she knew was that he couldn't possibly be seeing as well as usual. He couldn't hide that he was still shivering, too.

She watched as he staggered out of her sight to pee, returning a minute later. His usual grace had deserted him. How could they keep going? If they'd been on a smooth path or the road, maybe, but as it was...

How can we not *keep going?* Leah asked herself bleakly. It wasn't as if he had a twenty-four-hour flu bug. He wouldn't get better until he was on powerful antibiotics. If they didn't reach a hospital, he might die.

Even if they'd both been healthy, each day would be more grueling than the last, considering that they were able to drink only occasionally, and had nothing whatsoever to eat. It surely couldn't be that far before they reached the highway.

"You ready?" he asked gruffly.

Leah nodded. "Let me go first today."

He stared at her for long enough, she wasn't sure whether he was really slow in processing what she'd said, or resisting the idea. But finally, he nodded. Good.

She had to look around before deciding which way they'd come from, and therefore which way she needed to go. Some feature of ancient geology had formed a shallow dip here, and the forest was dense enough, she couldn't see very far ahead. As they started walking, her thighs let her know when the land tilted downward again.

Once, she said, "Oh, did you see that?" and turned, for a minute not seeing Spencer at all. Her heart took a huge, painful leap.

He plodded around the trunk of one of the forest giants. He hadn't heard her, and the small mammal she'd seen had long since dashed out of sight. His teeth were clenched, his eyes glazed, but he was able to keep moving.

No choice.

From then on she made sure to look over her shoulder regularly to be sure he was still with her.

The pace seemed awfully slow, but she felt sure that raw determination was all that kept Spencer moving.

A distant sound caught her attention. She grabbed Spencer's arm to stop him and listened, momentarily confused. That could be a river, but if it was the Nooksack, that meant they'd also reached the highway that followed it. Of course there were tributaries, like the one that flowed from the side of Mount Baker, running past the resort to meet the larger Nooksack, but the water didn't rush like—

It was a car engine. It had to be.

Traffic on the highway? Or had they unintentionally come close to the resort road?

Leah wished she could be sure where the sound came *from*, but her best guess at direction wasn't even close to precise. It wouldn't be so bad if they spotted the resort road, would it? At least they'd know where they were.

She glanced at Spencer, and fear gripped her. He looked bad. Really bad.

Maybe she should take the gun from him, start carrying it herself. If one of the men suddenly appeared in front of them, was Spencer capable of reacting quickly enough?

Could I? she asked herself, and was afraid she knew the answer. There was a reason cops and soldiers were supposed to spend so much time at gun ranges. *She'd* never fired a weapon in her life. To aim it at a person, one she knew, and pull the trigger— and that was assuming the gun didn't have a safety, which she had no idea how to identify.

Keep going. She had a very bad feeling that, if they took a break and sat down, she might have a hard time getting Spencer up again. She wouldn't be doing it with sheer muscle, since he had to outweigh her by eighty pounds, at least. There had to be a way…but he was still walking.

The light began to seem brighter ahead. They

emerged from the trees between one step and the next. Stumps and the kind of mess left by logging told her this land had been clear-cut, probably a couple of years ago. Some scruffy small trees grew, alder and maple, she thought. And a wealth of huckleberry bushes, many growing out of rotting stumps.

"Berries!" she cried.

Spencer bumped into her. For the first time in several hours, comprehension showed on his face. She steered him to a bush covered with purple-blue, ripe berries. Once she saw that he was able to pick them himself and stuff them into his mouth, she started doing the same.

They shouldn't eat very many; the last thing they needed was to end up sick, but oh, they tasted good, the flavor bursting on her tongue. And she was so hungry!

Within minutes her fingers were stained purple, as were Spencer's. But who cared?

Bushes a short distance away shook. Hand outstretched for more berries, Leah stared. It kept shaking, and that was an odd sound. Sort of…snuffling. Or grunting.

"Spencer," she whispered.

His head turned, his eyes sharp. He had to have heard the alarm in her voice.

He stared at the trembling leaves, and in a move so fast it blurred, had his gun in his hand.

"We need to back away," she murmured.

He nodded agreement.

"Probably won't pay any attention to us," she said, just as quietly.

A stick cracked under her foot. She'd have frozen in place if his hand hadn't gripped her upper arm and kept her moving.

Craning her neck, she saw brown fur. An enormous head pushed between bushes. Supposedly, bears didn't have very good vision, but it was staring right at them. And, oh, dear God, it kept pushing through the growth, canes snapping.

"Not too fast."

The bear wasn't charging, but Leah would have sworn it grew to fill her field of vision. Seeing the hump between the shoulders had her already racing pulse leaping.

"Spencer!" she whispered loudly.

"I see."

Another step, another. The head swung back and forth. Leah would swear the small eyes looked angry.

Suddenly, Spencer cursed, and she, too, heard a deep-throated engine cut off. Car doors slam.

"I see them!" yelled a voice she recognized and detested.

TJ Galt.

The racket off to the right made the bear even more agitated. It took a few steps toward them. Ignoring the two voices Leah now heard, Spencer held her to a slow, steady retreat.

Until the scrubby growth toward what had to be the resort road began to shake and snap as the men trampled through it. One of them yodeled, "Got you now, traitor!"

The grizzly lowered its head and charged.

"Run!" Spencer ordered. She didn't hesitate, racing as fast as she could back the way they'd come. It was a minute before she realized he'd split away, probably intending to draw the bear's attention.

But a gun barked. Again and again. TJ and Arne intended to shoot them down.

She heard a crashing behind her and dared a look back. The bear had stopped and swung toward the two men who were yelling gleefully. One took a shot at her that stung her arm. Spencer... She saw him trip, recover his footing and keep running.

The grizzly charged the men. One of them bellowed, "Bear!"

As if she'd stepped into a noose, Leah pitched forward. She didn't land gently, but didn't even acknowledge pain. Pushing herself to her hands and knees, she twisted to see what was happening.

Gunshots exploded but didn't slow the bear. Screaming, one of the men went down. The other stumbled backward. Even from this distance, she saw his horror.

"Keep going!" Spencer roared.

She used her position like a sprinter on a starting block to run, gasping, hurting, horrified by the snarls and terrible screams she heard behind her.

Leah hadn't gotten far into the woods when she slammed against a hard body. Even as she fought, she couldn't stop herself from looking back.

"Leah! It's me. It's just me."

She was whimpering as she took in his face. If she'd thought he looked bad before, it was nothing to now. He was as sickened as she was by what was happening behind them.

"Come on." He all but dragged her forward. She jogged to keep up with his long strides. Then she realized which hand he gripped her with.

"Your wrist."

"To hell with my wrist." He still held his gun in his right hand. "Let's circle around. If they both went down, we might have transportation."

The words were barely out of his mouth when the engine roared to life. Tires skidded on gravel as the driver floored it.

There was one more strangled scream.

SPENCER'S LUNGS HEAVED like old-fashioned bellows, and his heart was trying to pound its way out of his chest.

He and Leah had slid down an unexpected drop-off and collapsed at the bottom, their backs to a big tree.

She breathed as fast as he did, her eyes dilated, each exhalation sounding like a sob although she wasn't crying. "TJ," she gasped. "That was TJ."

"Yeah," he managed. "And Arne."

"He took off and left him." She sounded disbelieving.

He and she had taken off and left TJ to a terrible death, too, Spencer couldn't help thinking. They'd had more motivation to run even than Arne had, but Spencer also thought sticking around to try to rescue the grizzly's victim would have been useless and possibly a death sentence.

Shaking from reaction or the damn fever or both, he got out, "You okay?"

"I...don't know."

He wasn't a hundred percent sure he hadn't been shot. In fact, he bent his head to search for blood. He saw some, but on Leah, not him.

With an exclamation, he laid down his Sig Sauer and reached for her arm. "Does this hurt?"

She tipped her head to peer dubiously at the bloodstain on her upper arm. "Something stung me."

Yeah, there was a rip, all right. He parted it enough to see that the bullet had barely skimmed her flesh. Its passage might leave a scar, but the blood flow wasn't worrisome. Her face was decorated with some new scratches strung with beads of scarlet like polished rubies crossing her cheek and forehead.

He lifted a hand to smooth her hair, tangled with leaves and twigs. "Damn," he whispered. "I thought that was it."

"Me, too." She blinked against some moisture in her eyes. "TJ sneered at me when I said I was watching for bears. You know, when we were picking berries..."

"We'd better not stick around," Spencer said after a minute. As shitty as he felt, he wanted to kiss her, and maybe more. Nothing like a shot of adrenaline to fire up a man's blood and clear his head. Unfortunately, adrenaline didn't hang around long, and he'd crash when it dissipated. "That bear has to have taken a bullet or two. It'll be mad."

"It won't die?"

"I don't know. Not immediately, I'm guessing. Probably it just thinks it got stung by some yellow jackets."

Gutsy as always, Leah nodded sturdily. She got to her feet faster than he did and picked up his gun for him. Holstering it, he said, "I guess we found the road."

"Yes, and I'm pretty sure we're close to the turn-off."

"We still have to be careful, you know."

Her head bobbed. He had the feeling she was checking to see how *he* was, even as he did the same for her.

She looked like she'd been in a cat fight. Scratches, new and old, on her face and hands. Hair a mess. Her clothes, ripped and dirty, hung on her as if she'd already lost weight. Horror darkened her beautiful eyes.

He hadn't taken very good care of her.

They were alive, he reminded himself. Unlike TJ Galt.

An hour later they had circled around the clear-cut land and saw the resort road. It was paved here, which encouraged him. Not that far to go.

They hiked on, trying to move parallel to it, just near enough they could see it occasionally. Twice they saw a black SUV driving slowly along the road, once heading out, then coming back up.

"They still think they can cut us off," he said.

"What if the driver let off a couple guys who are on foot out here with us?"

The possibility was real, but there was nothing he could do that he wasn't already. He fought to stay in the moment while fighting a blinding headache, chills and a tendency to find himself in other times and places.

A kid, hiding in the woods near his house after his father had used his belt on him. Rage and fear and shame filled him. Sunlight in his eyes, and he was baking in the heat of a street between mud-colored buildings in a village in Afghanistan, feeling eyes on him from every direction. Skin crawling.

Turning his head to see Leah anchored him, so he kept doing it. She needed him. He couldn't let her down.

"I think I see someone," she whispered.

He stared hard in the direction she was looking. Yeah, that desert camo didn't quite work in the green northwest forest.

He nudged Leah, and they very, very quietly retreated, then turned east to parallel the highway, heading toward Mount Baker. Should have known they couldn't pop out right here. Had Higgs sent out his minions to drive up and down the highway, too? Should they hunker down and wait out the day, not try to flag anyone down until morning?

Might be safer…but Spencer bet that by morning, Higgs and the others would have decamped. He would very much like to round them up here and now.

Brooding, he thought, yeah, but what were the odds of getting a team here in time?

Even if the sheriff's department had a SWAT unit, could they stand up to the kind of weaponry Higgs's group had? An image formed in his head of the flare of rocket fire followed by a helicopter exploding.

He grimaced.

And, damn, as disreputable as he and Leah looked, how long would it take for police to be able to verify that he was who he said he was, and take action?

What if his head was in Afghanistan or Iraq when they reached a police station? Hard to take a crazy man seriously.

They trudged on, Leah in the lead again.

Her head turned. "I hear a car."

Pulled from the worries that had circled around and around, he listened, too. That was definitely a car, not an SUV or pickup. Which would have been good news if they'd been close enough to the highway to stick out a thumb. Also, if they could convince some backpacker on his way back down to civilization to hide them on backseat and floorboards so they weren't seen as they passed the resort road.

He realized he'd said that out loud when Leah said, "What if we *cross* the highway and follow it until we're past the resort road?"

It was lucky one of them had a working brain.

HER IDEA HAD sounded practical, but preparing to run across the empty highway, she was almost as scared as she'd been with a grizzly charging after her and bullets flying, too.

She and Spencer would be completely exposed for the length of time it took to slide into a ditch, climb up onto pavement, race across the highway and get across another ditch and into the woods on the far side. SUVs and pickup trucks with powerful engines could approach fast. Yes, but they could be heard from a distance, she reminded herself, even out of sight around a curve.

She stole an anxious look at Spencer. "Ready?"

"Yeah," he said hoarsely. "You say go."

"Okay." She took a few steadying breaths, tensed and said, "Go!"

Side by side, they slid on loamy soil into the ditch, used their hands to scrabble their way up to the road and ran.

Not until they plunged on the other side through dangling ropes of lichen and the stiff lower branches of evergreen trees did she take another breath. They stumbled to a stop, momentarily out of sight from the highway, and Spencer grinned at her.

Her heart gave a squeeze. That smile was delighted and sexy at the same time, and it didn't matter how awful he looked otherwise. When he held out his arms, she tumbled into them, wrapping her own around his lean torso.

She might have stayed longer if he didn't radiate worrisome heat.

"We're not safe yet," she mumbled into his shoulder.

"No, but we're one step closer."

Stupidly teary-eyed, she was smiling, too. Swiping her cheeks on his grungy T-shirt, she made herself lower her arms and back away.

"I don't know about you, but I'm starved. I vote we get going."

The jubilant grin had become an astonishingly tender smile. "I'll second that."

Chapter Seventeen

Two hours later they passed the turn-off to the resort without seeing a single vehicle or any camouflage-clad, armed men hiding in wait. They'd heard a fair amount of passing traffic, but chose not to attempt to stop anyone yet.

Their pace grew slower and slower. The trees weren't as large here, resulting in dense undergrowth. Leah's body had become more and more reluctant. Her legs didn't want to take the next step. She quit diverting to avoid getting slapped by branches. Stumbling, she'd barely catch herself before she did another face-plant. She had never in her life been so tired— and she didn't have a raging fever. She kept checking on him, sometimes slyly so he wouldn't notice. Despite a sheen of sweat on his face and glazed eyes, he plodded on.

Neither of them spoke. What was there to say?

Spencer glanced at his watch. She went on without bothering to ask what time it was. Occasional glimpses of the sun showed it still high enough to give

them a few hours before nightfall. If she was wrong…
they'd stop. Curl up together and sleep.

"Hey."

Hearing his rough voice, Leah didn't make her foot
move forward for that next step.

"Let's get in sight of the road. It's time to flag
someone down."

"Oh." How long had it been since she'd seen him
check the time? She had no idea. "Okay." She turned
right. Just the idea that they might catch a ride and
not have to walk anymore inspired a small burst of
energy.

It only took a few minutes—five?—to find themselves a spot to crouch barely off the highway, but
probably not visible to passing motorists.

The first one they saw coming was traveling east
toward Mount Baker. A red Dodge Caravan, it had
a rack piled with luggage and kids in the backseat.

They let several more go.

"I'd be happiest with a sheriff's deputy or forest
service," Spencer said.

Of course, they had to identify those quick enough
to give them time to burst out onto the road, waving
their arms and probably jumping up and down.

Vehicles passed. She began to wonder if Spencer
was too sick to make a quick decision. Maybe she
should make one.

But suddenly he said, "That's it," and launched
himself forward.

She stumbled behind, finally seeing what he had.
It was a white 4X4 with a rack of lights on the roof.

Spencer waved and so she did, too. A turn signal came on, and a siren gave a brief squawk. The vehicle rolled to a stop only a few feet from them. From here Leah could see green trim and the sheriff's department logo.

Spencer didn't wait for the deputy to get out. He jogged along the shoulder to the passenger side. So a passing motorist might miss seeing them, she realized.

The deputy climbed out and circled the front bumper. Probably in his thirties, he looked alarmingly like the men they were fleeing: fit, clothed in a khaki uniform and armed. In fact, his hand rested lightly on the butt of his gun.

That changed in an instant when he saw the gun holstered at Spencer's waist. In barely an instant, the deputy pulled his gun and took up a stiff-armed stance, the barrel pointing at Spencer, who immediately lifted his hands above his head. "Set that gun on the pavement," the deputy snapped. "Do it *now*."

Moving very slowly, Spencer complied. With his foot, he nudged the handgun over the pavement toward the cop. The deputy never took his eyes from Spencer when he moved forward and used his foot to push the gun behind the tire of his SUV.

"You're not a hunter."

"No," Spencer said. "I'm not carrying identification, so I can't prove this, but I'm FBI Special Agent Alex Barr. I was undercover with a violent militia group training at an old lodge near here. Ms. Leah Keaton—" he nodded at her "—recently inherited the lodge from her great-uncle. She decided to check on the condition of the buildings, and surprised the men who'd taken it over. They took her captive."

The guy watched them suspiciously. "You took her and ran?"

"Eventually. One of them found a photo of me on-line leaving a Chicago courthouse. We were lucky because Leah overheard two men talking about it. We didn't dare even take the time to grab supplies or my phone, just ran. I urgently need to call my team leader. These guys have some serious weapons, in-cluding a couple of rocket launchers."

"What?"

Leah spoke up. "I saw one of them. That's when they decided they couldn't let me leave."

"Some of their weapons are US military, stolen by a like-minded active-duty army officer. The leader of this group is a retired air force lieutenant-colonel. We need the FBI to handle this, not local police."

The deputy studied him for a long time. "No way I can verify this story."

"I don't see how."

Leah said, "The resort was called Mount Baker Cabins and Lodge. My uncle's name was Edward Preston. If you're local, you might know about him. He died last fall. I'm his great-niece. I'm…a veteri-nary technician."

The deputy eyed her. "We drove up to check on Mr. Preston now and again. Annoyed him, but we kept doing it."

"That sounds like him," she admitted. "Mom tried

to get him to move to somewhere less isolated, but he refused."

Looking marginally less aggressive, the deputy said, "Special Agent Barr, will you agree to be hand-cuffed before I give you and Ms. Keaton a lift?"

"Yes."

"He's wounded," she interjected desperately. "He has a knife wound in his thigh, and another between his ribs. I think the ribs are broken, and his wrist, too. He's fighting an infection."

The deputy's eyebrows rose and his gaze snagged on Spencer's wrapped wrist before moving to the blood soaking the upper arm of Leah's sweatshirt. "You appear to be hurt, too."

"Yes, I was shot, but it's just a graze. Spencer's wounds—I mean, Alex's wounds—are infected. He's running a high temperature. It's a miracle he made it this far. Please don't—"

"I'll be okay," Spencer said gently. "We need to get off this road."

He had to explain why she'd called him by two different names, and why it would be a bad thing if they were spotted by any of the men fleeing the lodge.

The deputy cast uneasy glances up and down the highway, patted them both down and made them sit in the back—in the cage, she thought was the right terminology—but didn't insist on the handcuffs. He took Spencer's gun with him when he got behind the wheel, and did an immediate U-turn to head west to-ward Bellingham and, presumably sheriff's depart-ment headquarters. Then he got on his radio.

LESS THAN TWO hours later Alex had set the ball to rolling. In his own imagery, he'd tapped a domino, which would knock down the next and the next, until the last fell.

He was rarely in on the grand finale, although his reasons this time were different. In the past, when he'd completed an undercover investigation, it was just as well not to show up days later as his alter ego, Special Agent Barr.

This wasn't the first time he'd had to jump ship, so to speak, but he'd never before had to help someone else make the swim to shore. It *was* the first time he'd been injured badly enough, he had to be hospitalized.

That partly explained his frustration. He did not like being stuck flat on his back in a hospital bed where he was allowed no voice in how the cleanup was run. He was pretty irked at Ron Abram, who'd delegated much of the response to someone at the Seattle office. Since Alex didn't have his phone, the only update offered to him came via the clunky phone on the bedside stand, and that was from Abram, not the agents who'd joined with the local police to raid the compound—yeah, that was what they'd called it—only to find it deserted. According to Abram, they were packing his and Leah's stuff and bringing it down, as well as having someone bring her car once they figured out how to get it moving.

Alex couldn't help thinking that Jason Shedd could have fixed the car in less time than it had probably taken him to disable it.

The Tahoe Alex had borrowed for this operation

from the Seattle office had started, once they recon-
nected the battery. No surprise it had been disabled.
He doubted they intended to return it to him. He
guessed he'd have to find his own way to the airport.

Truthfully, he still felt like crap, although the pain
meds had helped. He wouldn't be released until morning, at the very soonest. He was on some kind of su-
per-powerful antibiotic being given by IV, along with
the fluids the doctor thought he needed. They wanted
to see how he responded to the antibiotics before they
cut him loose.

What had him antsy was Leah's absence. He
wanted to rip the needle out and go looking for her.
They'd been taken to different cubicles in the ER and
he hadn't seen her since. There wasn't any chance
she'd been admitted, too, was there? He couldn't believe she'd leave without finding him. Anyway, she'd
need to wait for her purse and phone, even if she was
willing to abandon her car for now.

He'd tuned the TV to CNN, but had trouble caring
about the latest congressman embroiled in a sexual
scandal or tension in some godforsaken part of the
world. With a little luck Higgs and company would
be rounded up, weaponry confiscated and their entire scheme would become little more than a note on
a list of terrorist operations thwarted. No breathless
reports on CNN or any other news outlet.

Recognizing the quick, light footsteps in the hall,
he turned his head. Since hospital security had been
asked to vet any visitors to his room, he wasn't surprised to hear a man's voice and then a woman's. A

second later Leah pushed aside the curtain. Her hair was shiny clean and dry, shimmering under the fluorescent lights, and she wore scrubs.

"Spencer?" She sounded tentative, as if unsure he'd welcome her. Then she wrinkled her nose. "Alex."

"I'd really like to shed having multiple personalities," he told her.

She chuckled and visibly relaxed, coming to his side. When he held out his hand, she laid hers in it.

"Will you sit down?" he asked, tugging gently. The minute she'd perched on the edge of the bed, he said, "You saw a doctor. What did he say?"

She reported that, like him, she was being treated for potential *Giardia lamblia*, the microorganism commonly found in otherwise crystal-clear waters in the Cascade Mountains. A dressing covered the bullet graze on her arm, and she was also on an antibiotic for that. Otherwise, she'd been able to shower, a nurse had produced the scrubs for her and she'd been given a chit to pay for a meal in the cafeteria.

"I couldn't eat nearly as much as I wanted," she concluded ruefully.

With a smile lighting her face, she was different. Her eyes sparkled, her mouth was soft, her head high and carriage erect but also relaxed. Seeing her now was a reminder that he didn't know what she'd be like when she wasn't abused and shocked. She could have a silly sense of humor; she might be a party girl; she could habitually flit from one interest to another. Maybe she'd already dropped her determination to go to vet school and come up with another way she could spend any money earned from her great-uncle's legacy to her.

No, not that, he thought. That was unfair. He'd seen her unflagging determination. Her courage. Her strength and intellect.

Her smile had died, and she was searching his eyes gravely. "What about you? What did the doctor say?"

Was that the caring expression of a woman at least halfway in love with a man? Or caring only because the two of them had gone through a lot together?

"Nothing unexpected," he told her. "It was the gash on my thigh that was infected. Strangely enough, this one—" he started to move his free hand to touch his side before remembering that it was now casted "—appeared clean. One rib is broken, one cracked. My ulna is fractured close to the wrist." Rueful, he lifted the casted arm. "They expect a complete healing, but I may need physical therapy once this is off."

"I don't know how you kept going. You saved my life, over and over."

He shook his head. "You saved mine. Over and over."

She didn't seem convinced, and said, "Oh, you mean when I heard Higgs and Fuller talking."

"And when you treated my injures," he reminded her.

"Which you got because you were protecting *me*."

"You also knew enough to find berries to eat, to keep that bear from seeing us as dinner, and you led us to safety when I was too feverish to know which way we were going."

"I don't think any of those measure up to a knife to the—"

He smiled crookedly. "We'll call it even."

Leah laughed. "Not even close."

"Did anyone corner you with more questions?" he asked.

"Oh, yeah. A pair of FBI agents. Apparently, the doctor wouldn't let them go at you, so I got grilled instead."

He was the one to laugh this time. "Grilled?"

Her severe expression melted into a smile. "Okay, asked questions. Only…they wouldn't tell me anything. Do you know what's happening?"

The reminder renewed his irritation. "Not as much as I'd like. As we speculated, Higgs and his crew absconded with all the weapons, down to the last bullet." He told her the rest of what he'd learned, and she appeared relieved to know she'd get her possessions back soon.

"I was worrying about my car," she admitted. "I hated to have to call my insurance agent and say, 'Well, see, these domestic terrorists got mad at me, so they blew it up with a rocket launcher.'"

Laughing, Alex realized he hadn't felt this good since the last time he'd made love with Leah, and then the astonishing pleasure was transitory. They'd both been all too aware of the frightening reality awaiting them.

Before he could say anything else, he heard voices

in the hall, followed by one that said, "Knock knock," even as a hand drew back the curtain.

The visitor was Matt Sanford, the deputy who had picked them up off the side of the highway. He had a black duffel bag slung over one shoulder and was pulling a small suitcase with the other hand. "I thought you might like to have your stuff," he said cheerfully.

Leah beamed at him. "Yes, please. Is my purse there somewhere? You do have my phone?"

He let her seize the suitcase handle from him. "I'm told your purse is in the suitcase. The phone, I don't know. If anything is missing, I'll follow up on it." He looked at Alex. "And I take it this is yours."

"Well, the bag is."

"Do you want your phone?" Leah asked, starting to reach for the zipper.

"Eventually. Unfortunately, I don't dare use it until we know it's clean. Somebody was supposed to bring me—"

The deputy pulled a phone from a pocket. "I'm the somebody."

"Turned you into the pack mule, huh?"

"Beats my average day. You introduced some excitement into our lives."

Alex's eyes met Leah's. "More than I ever want to experience again."

"Amen," she murmured.

"Thank you," Alex added. "You don't know how glad to see you we were."

"That's what they all say," Deputy Sanford joked,

but he also smiled. "I'm happy I came on you when I did. Oh, I forgot to say I have an update."

Both focused on him.

"I hear the FBI has caught up with four men. A guy with a Scandinavian name..."

"Arne Larson?"

"That's it. He was with a Robert Kirk."

Leah's hand tightened on Alex's. "I don't remember a Robert."

Alex wasn't surprised. Unremarkable in appearance, Rob had never seemed interested in pushing himself forward.

"The other two were Don Durand—his truck was loaded with rifles, they said—and Garrett Zeigler."

"Those two were together?"

"Not from what I heard."

"I'm glad someone is willing to tell us what's happening."

"Yeah, I figured." Sanford sounded sympathetic. "I put my number in that phone. Call if I can do anything."

They expressed more thanks. He left, leaving silence in his wake.

THIS SILENCE FELT awkward to Leah. She wouldn't try to leave until morning at the soonest, Saturday if it looked like she'd have her car by then, but...should she hang around and keep Alex company now? Or make this breezy but plan to stop by in the morning to say goodbye?

Would she hear from him someday?

"I almost hope Del and Dirk get away," she blurted.

He grimaced. "Me, too, but that won't happen with Del. He got himself in too deep. Dirk… I'll try to keep him from being charged if he followed my advice."

He'd told her about the confrontation with Dirk and what he'd suggested. "If he didn't, there's not much I can do for him."

"How will you know?"

He ran a hand over his rough jaw. "As long as he doesn't have any stolen weapons on him when he's stopped, I'll assume he's running from Higgs, not still taking his orders. Dirk saved us by keeping his mouth shut."

Leah nodded. "They didn't let you shave?"

"Wasn't high on their list of priorities, but, damn it, I itch."

His disgruntlement made her smile. It also, for some obscure reason, made her sad. *Just ask*, she told herself.

"You'll be going back to Chicago, won't you?"

An emotion she couldn't read passed through his light gray eyes. "For the short term," he agreed. "I'm in no shape to be useful here."

"No. Um, I'm expected back at work Monday. So…"

"Have you talked to your parents?" he asked.

She scrunched up her nose. "Yes. Mom was next thing to hysterical. I could hear Dad in the background reminding her that I'm okay."

Annoyingly, amusement curved Alex's very sexy mouth. "Did you mention getting shot?"

Feeling sort of teenaged, she said, "I figured that could wait."

He laughed, but there was something intense in the way he watched her. "Leah…"

"Yes?"

"I don't want to say goodbye."

"I don't want to, either," she whispered, praying he didn't mean that in a "We had quite an adventure, and I'll miss you" way.

"Are you still serious about applying to vet school?"

"Yes, except…there's still the money issue. I suppose I should talk to some real estate agents tomorrow. It might be a while before they can actually take a look at the resort, though, huh?"

"I'm guessing a week or so," he agreed. His gaze never left hers. "I want to keep seeing you."

Her heart did a somersault. "But… Chicago."

"I'm done with undercover work. I can apply for a transfer to be near you."

He meant it. Suddenly, tears rolled down her cheeks. "I was so afraid…"

"I've been afraid, too," he said huskily, tugging her toward him.

Leah surrendered, lifting her feet from the floor so she could snuggle on the bed beside him, her head resting on his shoulder, her hand somewhere in the vicinity of his heart. The familiar position felt *right*. She hated the idea of going to bed without him.

"I had the terrifying thought that you might like nightclubs," he murmured.

She actually giggled at that. "Not a chance. Please tell me you don't bag a deer every year."

This laugh rumbled in his chest. "Nope. Guess that wouldn't go over very well with an animal doc, would it?"

"No." Her cheeks might still be wet, but Leah was also smiling.

"Now that we have that covered, I guess we know everything we need to about each other," he said with an undertone of humor.

"I guess we do." No, he wouldn't be able to go home with her to meet her parents immediately; she could only imagine the kind of debriefing he'd face. "Is there a Portland office?"

"FBI? Yeah, a field office. That's what I'll aim for in the short term. If you want me to."

"I do." She was in love with this man who was willing to make big changes in his life to be with her. The sexiest man she'd ever met. A man who just never quit.

"Good," he said. A minute later his breathing changed as he relaxed into sleep. Apparently, she'd removed his last worry.

Not planning to go anywhere, she closed her eyes, too.

Epilogue

Ten days later Alex strode off the plane at Portland International Airport. Leah had promised to be waiting for him at baggage claim. In part because of the cast he still wore, he carried only his laptop case. He'd taken a two-week vacation, the best he could manage until a transfer came through. This was a "meet the family" trip. Even as alienated as he often felt from his own parents, he supposed he'd be taking Leah to meet them one of these days, too. They loved him, if not in a way he'd want to replicate with his own kids. For the first time he was seriously thinking he'd like to start a family.

Only two days ago he'd gotten word that Higgs had been captured trying to charter a boat in Florida. When the local FBI located the beach cabin where he'd been staying, they'd surprised two other men: Steve Baldwin and Ken Vogel. They'd also found two rocket launchers and a small amount of uranium as well as evidence that the men had been constructing a bomb.

Higgs wasn't talking, but under pressure, Baldwin

admitted they'd intended to sail to a Caribbean island where they wouldn't be found until they were ready to make their strike.

Alex felt sick, imagining what might have happened if the charter operator hadn't had an uneasy feeling he'd seen Higgs's face, and not in a context he liked.

Yeah, the FBI had ended up putting Lieutenant Colonel Edward Higgs on a watch list, and released his photo. This time it had paid off big.

They had also quietly arrested army Colonel Thomas Nash, the man Alex recognized when he and Higgs met the suppliers. Turned out Nash and Higgs had been friends for years.

Of course, the single arrest was the equivalent of peeling open the proverbial can of worms. Nash couldn't have stolen that quantity of weapons on his own. Even with help, procedures were designed to prevent things like this from happening. It was fair to say that army base would be crawling with investigators for months to come, making a lot of people's lives miserable.

Dirk had been picked up and released, at Alex's recommendation. They'd spoken last week, Dirk shaken at his weakness in letting his father push him into something so hateful. He and Helen were getting married and moving to Montana, where he'd found a job with a well-drilling company based in Billings. Alex intended to stay in touch. He and Leah might not have survived if Dirk hadn't listened to his conscience.

Suddenly, he didn't want to think about any of that.

The baggage claim carousels were just ahead…and his gaze locked on a woman hurrying toward him, her face alight. Relief and something more powerful flooded him. He let the laptop case drop to the floor and held out his arms.

Leah flew into them, saying only his name. His real name.

* * * * *

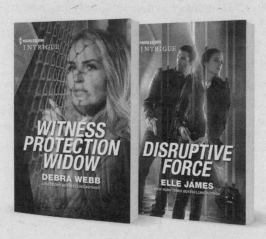

COMING NEXT MONTH FROM

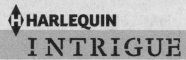

INTRIGUE

Available December 29, 2020

#1971 IMPACT ZONE
Tactical Crime Division: Traverse City • by Julie Anne Lindsey

TCD special agent Max McRay is the definition of *unflappable*. But when a serial bomber wreaks havoc in the town where his ex-wife, Allie, and infant son live, suddenly a high-profile case becomes personal.

#1972 HOMICIDE AT WHISKEY GULCH
The Outriders Series • by Elle James

When Delta Force soldier Trace Travis returns home after his father's murder, he partners with Lily Davidson, his high school sweetheart, to find his father's killer—and overcome the circumstances that have always kept them apart.

#1973 AGENT UNDER SIEGE
The Justice Seekers • by Lena Diaz

The police believe they have found Teagan Ray's kidnapper, but Teagan knows they're wrong. Former profiler Bryson Anton agrees to investigate, but soon their search results in brutal attacks from a cunning suspect...and a powerful mutual attraction.

#1974 THE FUGITIVE
A Marshal Law Novel • by Nichole Severn

When Raleigh Wilde reappears in Deputy Beckett Foster's life asking for his help to clear her name, he's shocked—even more so when he learns she's pregnant with his child. But a killer is willing to do anything to keep Raleigh from discovering who embezzled millions from the charity she runs...

#1975 DEAD MAN DISTRICT
The Taylor Clan: Firehouse 13 • by Julie Miller

Firefighter Matt Taylor's new neighbor, Corie McGuire, makes Matt want to focus on the present. Her troubled son, Evan, reminds Matt of his younger self. When the boy is implicated in a string of fires, Matt vows to help. Is Evan guilty...or has Corie's past come back to threaten them all?

#1976 ALASKA MOUNTAIN RESCUE
A K-9 Alaska Novel • by Elizabeth Heiter

Alanna Morgan was raised by kidnappers in remote Alaska. But now she's hunting for her criminal "mother" with Peter Robak, a cop who trusts her as little as she trusts him. As they investigate, she and Peter begin to move past old traumas to deeply connect...while danger looms at every turn.

YOU CAN FIND MORE INFORMATION ON UPCOMING HARLEQUIN TITLES, FREE EXCERPTS AND MORE AT HARLEQUIN.COM.

HICNM1220

Raleigh Wilde.

Hell, it'd been a while since Deputy United States Marshal Beckett Foster had set sights on her, and every cell in his body responded in awareness. Four months, one week and four days to be exact. Those soul-searching light green eyes, her soft brown hair and sharp cheekbones. But all that beauty didn't take away from the sawed-off shotgun currently pointed at his chest. His hand hovered just above his firearm as the Mothers Come First foundation's former chief financial officer—now fugitive—widened her stance.

"Don't you know breaking into someone's home is illegal, Marshal?" That voice. A man could get lost in a voice like that. Sweet and rough all in the same package. Raleigh smoothed her fingers over the gun in her hand. It hadn't taken her but a few seconds after she'd come through the door to realize he'd been waiting for her at the other end of the wide room.

It hadn't taken him but a couple hours to figure out where she'd been hiding for the past four months once her file crossed his desk. What she didn't know was how long he'd been waiting, and that he'd already relieved that gun of its rounds as well as any other weapons he'd found during his search of her aunt's cabin.

"Come on now. You and I both know you haven't forgotten my name that easily." He studied her from head to toe, memorizing the fit of her oversize plaid flannel shirt, the slight loss of color in her face and the dark circles under her eyes. Yeah, living on the run did that to a person. Beckett unbuttoned his holster. He wouldn't pull. Of all the criminals the United States Marshals Service had assigned him to recover over the years, she was the only one he'd hesitated chasing down. Then again, if he hadn't accepted the assignment, another marshal would have. And there was no way Beckett would let anyone else bring her in.

Beckett ran his free hand along the exposed brick of the fireplace. "Gotta be honest, didn't think you'd ever come back here. Lot of memories tied up in this place."

"What do you want, Beckett?" The creases around her eyes deepened as she shifted her weight between both feet. She crouched slightly, searching through the single window facing East Lake, then refocused on him.

Looking for a way out? Or to see if he'd come with backup? Dried grass, changing leaves, mountains and an empty dock were all that were out there. The cabin she'd been raised in as a kid sat on the west side of the lake, away from tourists, away from the main road. Even if he gave her a head start, she wouldn't get far. There was nowhere for her to run. Not from him.

"You know that, too." He took a single step forward, the aged wood floor protesting under his weight as he closed in on her. "You skipped out on your trial, and I'm here to bring you in."

"What was I supposed to do?" Countering his approach, she moved backward toward the front door she'd dead-bolted right after coming inside but kept the gun aimed at him. Her boot hit the go bag she stored near the kitchen counter beside the door. "I didn't steal that money. Someone at the charity did and faked the evidence so I'd take the fall."

"That's the best you got? A frame job?" Fifty and a half million dollars. Gone. The only one with continuous access to the funds stood right in front of him. Not to mention the brand-new offshore bank account, the thousands of wire transfers to that account in increments small enough they wouldn't register for the feds and Raleigh's signatures on every single one of them. "You had a choice, Raleigh. You just chose wrong."

Don't miss
The Fugitive *by Nichole Severn,*
available January 2021 wherever
Harlequin Intrigue books and ebooks are sold.

Harlequin.com

HIEXP1220

Get 4 FREE REWARDS!

We'll send you 2 FREE Books plus 2 FREE Mystery Gifts.

Harlequin Intrigue books are action-packed stories that will keep you on the edge of your seat. Solve the crime and deliver justice at all costs.

FREE Value Over $20